From the Author

People no longer read what the author has to say before diving right into the book; they no longer want to know where the stories and ideas are come from.

I came to the realization that writing is the only thing that may bring me peace after completing my first and second books, (*She Had It All* and *Tides Of The Past*). I made the decision to become involved with more true stories and write about the highs and lows of real people's lives.

Since I had made the decision to keep writing, it was too embarrassing for me to stop people and inquire about their personal lives, and I had no idea where to start.

My love for writing persisted even after I made the decision to continue my nursing degree. I made the decision to put in extra hours at the start of my term and save some pocket money for costs.

When I contacted one of our family friends for assistance, she suggested I work at a desk in the psychology clinic. I can learn a lot there, she claimed, and I can get paid as well.

As soon as they noticed I was new and fresh, they started assigning me anything, including making coffee for physicians and ordering breakfast, helping the cleaning staff, and making sure the restrooms were always spotless. It was harder than I had anticipated, and I hoped it was just a desk job. However, I was required to gather information about anyone who wished to attend the free group and individual treatment sessions that our clinic was providing.

After a time, I realized that many of the young people were more interested in chatting to me than the other members of the team. They were interested in learning more about me, and as they were more at ease, they began telling me some of their history, which was wonderful.

Some of them learned about my love of writing, and I even read my most recent two works to them. I choose Ariana's narrative with the clinic's and the story's owner's consent.

My stories are not particularly impressive or filled with surprises for the reader, but they are all true and have already had an impact on someone's life. Each person has a unique story to tell.

I consider myself extremely fortunate to have had the opportunity to write her narrative.

I sincerely hope you'll like reading my third novel.
And remember, I love you all.

—Yalda

The life is more valuable with you three in it; thus, this is dedicated to Chanake, Anusheh and Aniseh.

—Yalda

Yalda Afshoon

Silver Skies and Stars

Inspiring Real-life Story and Unfulfilled Desires

AUSTIN MACAULEY PUBLISHERS™

LONDON ★ CAMBRIDGE ★ NEW YORK ★ SHARJAH

ISBN 9789948792185 (Paperback)
ISBN 9789948792192 (E-Book)

Application Number: MC-10-01-7415197
Age Classification: 17+

Printer Name: iPrint Global Ltd
Printer Address: Witchford, England

First Published 2023
AUSTIN MACAULEY PUBLISHERS FZE
Sharjah Publishing City
P.O Box [519201]
Sharjah, UAE
www.austinmacauley.ae
+971 655 95 202

Tables of Contents

Chapter 1
Raw Sienna

In the quiet room, I could only hear Mr. Allen, our history lecturer, moving around and checking each student's responses on the exam sheet.

I was repeating the response to myself. I was still thinking about the previous question. I had no idea why I struggled to retain the information from the Tudors course.

The time was up and we had to turn in our papers, so I had to get it all perfect if I didn't want to lose any points. I glanced across at Sicilia, who had a large smile on her face despite the fact that I was dissatisfied with the outcome and knew she had correctly answered every question.

This time, I'll let her have it, I told myself.

I should not be disappointed because I just lost one point, Mr. Allen said as he accepted my papers. I told him, "Please provide more multiple questions next time," as I gave him a lengthy stare, as if it were his fault.

In order to modify my mood a little bit during the break, I also got up and left the class.

While grinning broadly, Sicilia declared that she would receive full marks for the last three tests. I was so angry that I could easily have shattered every window in the security room in front of me!

I made an effort to calm myself down by reminding myself that the finals, which were rapidly approaching, would be the occasion for me to demonstrate my talent to Sicilia.

"Ariana, Ariana, where are you, girl? I've looked all over for you."

My sole friend in the entire school, Catherine, was there. Since kindergarten, we have been friends. She never had a sense of style; she would wear whatever she found in her drawers! Particularly when she was about to pay us a visit.

Why was she seeking me out so fervently, I questioned her. Did you know that the high school graduate with the best grade would receive a scholarship for college? She grabbed my hand and led the way as she led me aside.

She continued, "The university, which is located in the city, has given chance to the female students in the small town by creating such an opportunity for them; the best part is that they will only pick one, and they will cover all the cost as well, including three meals a day and accommodation they will provide!"

I began to picture myself as the fortunate one, but Sicilia was also around, so it was too early to start daydreaming. I reminded myself that I must put in more effort if I want to take advantage of this chance.

I believe Catharine had the same notion for me when she informed me that, in addition to my high-test score, I can also easily get into the university because I am skilled in swimming, basketball, and writing.

As soon as she started a subject, she won't stop unless someone or anything stops her, so I told her let's go to class before we both get marked as being absent.

She began complimenting me as we were making our way to the lesson and said she would now depend on me.

I pleaded with her to cool off and stop being so excited. When I pinched Catherine, she leapt out of her seat and said, "Present, Ms. Julie," despite the fact that Ms. Julie had already started calling for the register.

She was acting in such a way that the entire class was laughing!

I was not at all hungry when I arrived home that day, but my mother asked me to change and come for lunch. I enquired as to her where my younger brother Adam was.

According to her, he got into an argument with his mates as usual, and because he wasn't feeling well, he shut himself in the room. "He is still unaware that he cannot rule the world by fighting and arguing!" I said.

My mom advised me to finish my lunch and keep my thoughts to myself.

She didn't want anyone to talk negatively about Adam because she treated us in a very different way from how she treated Adam, whom she even respected as a little boy. My mother contacted me as I was leaving for my room to tell me that she has invited some visitors for tonight and wanted my assistance. I couldn't finish my lunch, so I wiped the table and did the dishes.

When I told her I had an exam coming up tomorrow, she remarked, "I am weary of the excuses you usually create to avoid helping me. There are plenty other important things in our lives besides studying and tests, so attending school no longer makes sense…”

She brought out a large bundle of fruits and veggies, instructed me to wash them and arrange them attractively on a crystal tray, boil the potatoes, and begin creating the special mash gravy that would go with the steak as a side dish.

Because I knew what would happen if I refused, I was unable to deny her.

I therefore followed her instructions exactly. Still unsure of who she had invited, she abruptly revealed that my aunt Rose hadn't visited our home in a while and that she had thought to invite them.

After I completed everything in an hour, she asked me to clean the home and wash the balcony. I informed her that I had a crucial exam the next day, so might I spend a little time reading before returning to finish the remainder and helping her?

I should stop thinking about going to school starting tomorrow, she said if I mentioned the exam and studying one more time.

She then began yelling, “As a girl, you need to focus on housework, baking, sweeping, laundry, and maintaining the family as a whole, and that is it.”

She even remarked that I was extremely fortunate to still be in school because so many females my age have already had their first child and are expecting their second, which was true.

When I finished working after hearing what she had to say, she asked me to keep some fruit and veggies for my grandma and bring them downstairs.

I hurriedly packed some for her and sprinted downstairs because this work never ended.

My older sister Arta, who was married and lived with her family on the third floor of our three-story apartment, and was on the first floor, my grandmother. My grandpa owned the entire structure, and granny was initially in charge after his passing.

I waited patiently after knocking because I knew it would take her about 10 minutes to answer.

She was always grouchy and took her time opening the door. She instructed me to wash my hands before handling anything and to save anything my mother provided in the kitchen so she could inspect it later.

Each month, we all paid my grandma's rent as her tenants. She was fairly large in stature and had very long, white colored hair that she hardly ever combed or washed.

I inquired about her activity because the house was unusually quiet. She became irate and yelled, "Your mother sent you here to find out what I'm doing. Can't she quit meddling in my life?"

She did not even take the time to say thank you. Asked me to start cleaning the kitchen for her since I was already there. There were many plates, cups, and spoons that needed to be washed. I opened the refrigerator because I couldn't stand the smell; I believe there was food inside that had been spoiling for days but hadn't even been bothered to throw it out.

I felt like I hadn't had a single break from this family's issues in order to study for my upcoming exam.

She requested me to brush her hair after I was finished, and as I was doing so, I wondered why, ten years after Grandpa's death, she hadn't yet packed his clothes. Everything in their room remained the same, and I couldn't tell if this was because she loved him so much or was simply too lazy to clean it.

She responded, "I can't manage two sons-in-law in one night, tell Reena (my mother) and her sister (Rose) to come and visit me after dinner and this time bring warm food not the frozen food," when I invited her to join us for dinner after brushing her hair.

She was quite bossy, and her daughters were much like her. I assured her that I would send along her instructions to the girls, and she asked if I was finished cleaning before I left because it was beyond her nap time and she needed to rest.

Father was watching his favorite football game on TV when I said hello and promptly made plans to retire to my room. He then requested that I bring a cup of coffee!

I entered the kitchen as my mother was cooking some potato chips and she instructed me to come back and wash the dishes after I served him coffee.

Around seven o'clock in the evening, I was still at work and had no opportunity to go to my room and study.

As I poured the coffee for my father, I noticed Adam cutting some paper and attempting to fold a dragon. I ordered him to stop making the hallway dirty again, he threw the scissors my way, and I lost control of my balance and dropped the coffee mug. My mother ran out and yelled at me, telling me how clumsy I was and incapable of doing anything well!

I hurriedly wiped the floor and made another coffee for him.

The bell rang, and my aunt and her family had already arrived. I was unable to even get dressed.

Then there was Rasoul, who attended the same school as Adam and was wearing jeans and a blue t-shirt. Aunt Rose was wearing a very short yellow dress with full makeup and clutching her husband's hand as she entered. Rika, her daughter, was the same age as Arta but was already separated.

They were a loud, untidy family who made a lot of noise. Aunt Reena was telling my mother that although they had been prepared since five, they had decided to stop at the park on route. They had been on the swing while her husband Neal, and they had both played and enjoyed themselves immensely before going to our house a little later.

Uncle Neal was attempting to win his wife over by telling her that she was still very slim and stunning like the day he had first met her.

Rika was trying to convince her father that she had gained weight and that her clothing no longer fit her, but it appeared that my aunt was unhappy with what she was saying and was trying to keep her daughter silent.

Last week, Aunt Rose claimed that during a party, her friends had questioned her about how she managed to keep so young and attractive. They had inquired about her age rather than her fitness, Rika said while grinning.

Mother tried to change the subject and gave them some fruit to assist themselves with when I believe everyone was growing bored.

Rika questioned, "How are you? Are you studying so hard to obtain As in every class?" as she turned to face me. Rasoul and Adam started giggling at her query.

My mother instructed me to go to the kitchen and begin setting the dinner table when I wanted to respond to her.

I set the table up properly and then requested my mother to come serve the meal as I was not allowed to do it myself.

While Dad and uncle were playing chess in the hallway, Aunt Rose was trying to grab everyone's attention by mentioning the new gold set that her husband had given her the previous week.

Next week's party was going to be a huge one, and only the wealthy were invited, according to Aunt Rose, who asked my mother if she may come along. Ms. Elsa, the party's host, had told her to bring whomever she liked.

Then Rika pleaded with my mother not to bring awkward Ariana because I would make a fool of myself in front of everyone. My mother didn't even bother to respond to Rika before saying that she hadn't attended a major party in a long time and should search her closet to see what she could find.

Everyone ate their meals when the food was provided, but I was left to do all the cleaning, as per usual.

After dinner, it was time for dessert. Mother didn't give me a chance to even finish my meal because she kept telling me what to do while she sat next to other women and discussed what to wear, the best color shoes to go with her dress, and what jewelry was the most eye-catching. It was as if she had hired a maid.

I told my mother that Grandmother wanted to see them; she berated me for not mentioning it earlier, and Rika retorted that I was stupid and incapable of doing anything correctly. Rika had a wonderful figure despite her lack of beauty. I struggled to understand why she never regarded me as a relative.

How difficult it must have been for them to respect me and how come any of them didn't genuinely know me! I went to my room after they eventually departed and collapsed on my bed. I decided to take a quick shower to wake up and get ready. I studied for four hours after getting dressed, and I believe I was done studying material around three in the morning.

Only two hours of sleep were possible that night.

Chapter 2
Olive Green

There were only two high schools in our area, and the one for girls had just recently been built.

The main town was two hours away from our location. Regrettably, the cultures of those living in the big city and those in the small towns were very different.

My sister Arta married at the age of fifteen, and my cousin Rika was divorced twice by the time she was twenty, so I assume my town was the worst and it seems ladies were not permitted to have a life once they were sixteen.

The exam wasn't too tough, but I wasn't sure whether I would receive full marks. I noticed Sicilia was really delighted after receiving full marks, and the teacher walked over and questioned why I should be grinning when my scores were higher than hers.

After what happened to me yesterday, I suppose I was extremely fortunate to be able to attend school at all.

During the break, Sicilia approached me and said, "Don't try too hard, I can see you are already seated in the losers' section. My parents have engaged five tutors for different subjects, and they want me to get the most attention. I am confident I will be the one who gets into university."

When I returned home, I discovered Arta in our home. When I asked her where Mom was, she replied that she had taken grandma to the clinic for her checkup. Arta then proceeded to ask a zillion questions about last night, including how Rika's style was, what she was wearing, what color her nails were, and which brand of handbags she carried.

Sincerely, I didn't notice any of those, and I simply replied that I wasn't paying attention. She grew impatient and said, "You are really incredibly dumb as others are saying, when are you starting to understand, the only stuff matters is the style and brand names these days, even skilled people are running after that."

She forbade me from entering my room because her daughter Analia was sound asleep on my bed, but I didn't mind. I grabbed my book and headed to the balcony to study.

After my mother arrived two hours later, I was so relieved to have finished my studies that I promised myself that I would examine everything one more time that night to make sure I had understood it.

Mother was busy discussing the upcoming party to which aunt Rose had invited them with Arta and bringing different clothes from her closet for them to try. Later, she told Arta to go to our family tailor order a lovely gown for herself before it was too late, and she wanted me to watch Analia until she returned. When Mom gets home, I know she won't let me in and will find a way to offer me something and distract me from my schoolwork.

Analia had just turned three and was constantly grumpy; I was the only one with whom she felt at ease. Till her mother returned, I made every effort.

Mom never stopped gushing about Ms. Elsa's birthday party, the number of city residents who were invited, and how fortunate we were to be able to join.

"Arta fell in love, now she is having a baby too, although her husband is not what we expected but she was lucky to find someone to marry her," she continued, making a serious look as she motioned for Arta and I to sit on the sofa. Mother added, "From now on, I want you Arianna to join all the events, this is the first one and you need to be the star of the show."

With only a few months remaining till I start university; you will see me traveling to a huge city for my education. I rose up and begged her to support me and not include me in this disgusting business.

You may easily find a rich and affluent husband in one of these parties, Mom added after pushing me to the seat. "You just need to be more sociable and attractive. Boys will kill for you."

She was informed by Arta that since I was just sixteen and the time had changed, it might be best not to rush.

She requested that she refrain from interfering and let her do what she felt was best for the family.

She advised me to start studying some moves from Arta so that I wouldn't act foolishly in front of any guys.

I assured her that if she lets me attend college once I graduate, I will undoubtedly meet a decent boy who has a similar education to mine, and perhaps we will tie the knot at that point.

She told me it was ridiculous of me to search for a husband for such a long time when one was right in front of me.

As the first child in her family, my mother was asked to stop attending school at the age of twelve by her military-serving father in order to stay at home and begin studying new things in order to prepare for her future. She received a large amount of housework to complete.

My father, who at the time was the single baker in our town, witnessed my mother, falling in love with her. The next day, they announced their engagement, and a month later they were married.

The tale of Aunt Rose was entirely different; she was married to the son of her painting teacher. She never intended to go to school, and she will give birth to her first child just after getting married!

A long, white, silky garment that Arta claimed she could find for me in her closet is now too small for her after being worn just once.

Mom was overjoyed that I could attend the party and at least have a dress.

I lost my patience and went to get my English book while announcing that I was going downstairs to see grandmother.

Grandma answered the door when I knocked; she had unkempt hair as usual and questioned why I had a book in my hand yet again.

She let me in after I explained what was going on upstairs and said she was alright with me staying to study as long as I didn't bother her.

After kissing her, I entered the reading room, which was packed with used copies of books of all genres, especially novels.

I started going over the lectures again to make sure I understood everything. Grandma welcomed me to use the library room whenever I need it.

I gave her another kiss and questioned why my mom is so opposed toward education.

She sat down at the table and declared, "She was always in a hurry, even when she was young. I know in earlier days study did not have a place for a woman, but now it has changed, and Reena (my mother) wants to claim the

Kilimanjaro Mountain during the course of a single night." She continued after asking me to give her some medications.

Rose was much better, but she disliked limits, which is why she continues to dress in those ways and her daughter imitates her. She and her husband are both enjoying themselves, but nobody seems to mind because they are both content. As their mother, I don't want to meddle in their lives, but on the other hand, I am saddened by what they are doing to my granddaughters, so I have stayed away from both of my children. I wish her a good night and walked out.

I returned to my room and lay on my bed contemplating what Grandma had said. She was an intelligent woman, but why had she allowed Grandpa to let the girls be married at such a young age? Perhaps she was too afraid to ask him as she was much years younger than him!

I just drift off to sleep without eating dinner.

Chapter 3
Peach

I informed Mother, "This is the first and last time, and I won't be joining any of these absurd gatherings."

"I'm sure that after today, you will be going to all the parties. All the ladies are like that, they don't feel confidence at first, but once you discover what or how you should perform and look, you will enjoy it," she offers her opinion.

I put on Arta's dress, which was a little too long for me. She then applied makeup; I was uncomfortable, but my mother pushed.

I only permitted them to use lipstick and mascara, and I requested her to leave my hair open.

I was shocked to see myself in the mirror because I had never paid attention to how attractive I was. I had dark brown hair that was somewhat wavy, I was tall and skinny, and my mother had always said that my lips were larger than they should be. I wasn't sure whether this was a good or bad thing.

I was proud of myself and thought *after all, it is not bad to be a girl sometimes and dress as one.*

When I asked my mother about Dad, Grandma, and Adam, she replied that everything was in order and there was no need to worry. Dad would not be coming because he had stated that this was not his place, Adam had invited his friends over for a game night, and Grandma was going to visit an old friend who lived nearby. With her spouse, Arta was raising her daughter.

Dad not coming along upset me because this was the perfect opportunity for my parents to bond, dance, and have some leisure time together.

"Shouldn't we pick up Dad?" I queried.

"Let the old man be in his bakery and keep content with his buns," my mother commanded. "He won't let us do anything, won't even let you chat to any boys if he comes, and what about dancing with them?"

She brought me, but she took our dad out of tonight's presentation! I couldn't believe it! Even the dance had been prepared by her. I promised myself that I wouldn't dance with anyone under any circumstances.

"Who is taking us there, then?" asked Arta.

"You're a fool like Ariana too, of course my sister will," Mom answered.

Despite what she had informed us, Rose showed up a little earlier than expected. I believe they were both dressed in bridal gowns, and seeing them made me anxious because I wasn't sure where we were heading.

Rika remarked that it was nice to see me out of my uniform before we all climbed in their car. However, Arta and I were unable to find a room because Rika and her gown took up the entire back row.

When Rose began to drive, she was heading at the highest speed ever, and we were all hoping that nothing would go wrong before we arrived.

"Are guys invited, or are only women, Mom?"

"Naturally darling, a gathering without males is no fun," Rika's mother responded to her question.

The mansion was so large that it took us a half-hour to get there. I couldn't believe real people actually owned such a massive house. There were five gates and valet parking available.

I started to get afraid and really wanted to stay in the car till they returned, but it seemed like there were no other options.

The lads and girls, who were both wearing impeccable suits and stunning outfits, were dancing together on stage. When I noticed a lovely woman approaching us, Rose stepped over to shake her hand before leading the way. She then gave me a serious look and remarked, "Rose, you never mentioned that you have beautiful nieces, particularly this one."

After asking my name and hearing 'Ariana,' she drew closer and added, "Most holy, flawless name, matching with your beauty and pure look, I loved to introduce you to my son." When we arrived at the table, which was already set aside for Aunt Rose and her guests, she instructed us to discover our names.

Although very crowded, everything was nicely organized. When Arta began to eat from every item that was placed on our table as an appetizer, Mother asked her to restrain herself.

At the end of the hallway, I overheard Rose chatting to a middle-aged, confident man who was dressed in black pants, a red shirt, and a black tie.

When Mom noticed that I was gazing at them, she added, "Your aunt will break Mr. Jack's heart and marry Neal because she couldn't be without a man, even for a month! Mr. Jack was Rose's first sweetheart, and he would travel for a month with his family in the summer. Since Neal and Jack were also great friends, sharing their affection was acceptable to them. Your aunt calls this being open-minded."

"Rose loves to attend all the events," Arta said, "possibly because she is tracing Jack's footsteps."

"Don't be shocked if these two mysteriously vanish in this crowd, they have a lot to catch up on," said Mom.

Mother stood up in respect as we saw Ms. Elsa heading in our direction. She then asked if she might take me with her and introduce me to her son Edwin.

Mother was overjoyed; she didn't even ask my opinion; she just held my hand and shouted, "She is all yours!" while holding Ms. Elsa's hand.

Because of my lengthy dress and ill-fitting high heels, I struggled to breathe and made an effort to move gently. She thought I'm too nervous to walk with her, so she slowed down as well.

She was welcoming the many individuals who had stood up in front of her as she walked while also requesting that they assist themselves.

Ms. Elsa studied in France, taught art, and had a husband who was one of the most powerful merchants. Although they were from our town, you hardly ever saw them because their first home was in Paris. In my brief existence, she was one of the most powerful women I had ever seen. She was frequently assisting women and was regularly becoming involved in charitable projects.

"Your cousin doesn't have any boundaries," she said, pointing at Rika who was dancing with a boy named Harold. "No one in this hall was ready to dance with Harold after he had done to his wife. Everyone is scared of him and the way he is treating women."

Her son was also seated at the bar in the corner of the room when she yelled loudly, "Edwin," and he turned to face us after turning back to see what she was calling for. With his tall stature, muscular frame, tan skin, and green eyes, he truly resembled the models on magazine covers.

I don't know what happened, but I abruptly stopped moving. She went up to him and said, "Look what I discovered, a beautiful red diamond; her name is Ariana; can you believe it; in this tiny town, you can find model like her?"

She left us alone, and seeing that I was still standing, I assume he saw me and pulled over a chair, offering me a seat. We both sat quietly, staring at the dance stage.

He wasn't paying attention to me, so I decided it would be best to leave. After I apologized and he asked if someone was waiting for me (I replied that there wasn't), he asked what I liked to drink, to which I replied that a glass of water will do.

We weren't sure why we were both staring at Rika and Harold.

"It's unfortunate that some individuals still can't tell the difference between a dance stage and a bedroom," Edwin stated as he turned to face me.

I was extremely ashamed of Rika's actions and his remark.

Edwin made a statement about how young I looked, and when I informed him I was sixteen and intended to attend college, he laughed.

This time, he didn't attempt to stop me when I immediately excused myself and went to our table, where my mother and sister were seated and prepared to ask a hundred questions.

My mother asked me why I left so early while I was exhausted and quite worried, and when I told her about his remark, she replied, "I knew you were a failure, Rika likes to be this way, what does it have to do with us?"

"They are the ones who brought us here, Rose is disappeared with Mr. Jack, and Rika is wasted and dancing on the stage with the wicked guy. Thus, it is clear that they believe we are similar to them," I said. Mother was so angry.

I was not even interested in watching what was happening when I observed Edwin ask his mother to be his dance partner. I sat down and turned so that I wouldn't see him.

When I asked Arta if there was a way I could take a taxi home, she grinned and replied, "If I were you, I wouldn't come to this party no matter what; sadly, you were not strong enough in front of Mom. You have stayed to the very end."

I'm not sure why, but I believe I noticed tears in her eyes because this was the first time, I noticed her speaking about Mother in this way.

Everyone was asked to supper, which was served in the garden, by Ms. Elsa. What a gorgeous outdoor space! It was decorated in a really romantic manner with many lights that were tucked away in the countless rose plants. Food was being served all around the pool.

The manner in which all of those dressed-up folks were lining up made it seem as though they were just discovering food! Some of them were using the same dish twice. Who knows, perhaps they were just like us and dressed to impress while having nothing in their pockets.

Since I wasn't hungry, I chose to sit and observe the others. I noticed a guy who had been staring at me the entire time walking toward me, and when he asked to join me, I just answered, "No problem."

He grinned and sat down, then added, "I'm Zack, and I'm the conductor of the town orchestral. There is no music in the world that I cannot play. How are you doing? Do you have any music going?"

I was wondering why he was saying this stuff to me. I then noticed my mother was glancing at me from a distance. I realized he might be one of her contenders, so I had to act appropriately.

I just said, "Wonderful, you're extremely skilled, and No, I don't play any music," in response.

"No problem, I'm here to teach you, and may I please have the honor of dancing with tonight's most stunning girl," he said.

Oh my goodness, I've never danced before, not even once. How am I going to make it? He repeated his words once again while I was thinking to myself, but this time he held my hand.

Sadly, I agreed. After he looked at the musicians and I assume they knew which song was his favorite, they began to play. Other than us, no one else had planned to dance during dinner. We both got up and walked over to the dance floor. I'm not sure why I agreed to his offer when I could have said no.

Do as I do, he said as he held me motionless in his own presence with one hand around my waist.

I believe he was aware that this was my first time, so I followed his lead. The nicest thing was that he was purposefully moving slowly so I could keep up with him.

It made me more anxious that Edwin was constantly watching us when he said, "It was fantastic for the first time, your body was so smooth and warm in my palm, shall we look for a room?" when we were dancing. Everyone was looking at us, and I was sure he was expecting me to act like Rika. I was so angry that I smacked him and left the stage with a sorrowful face.

First to arrive to observe what was happening was Arta, followed by Mom, Rose, and Rika.

Mother questioned me, "What was wrong with me, why did I act so foolishly in front of everyone?"

"He is a gentleman; how could you exhibit such a fitting response?" asked Rika.

When I told them what a shameful thing he had asked me, Rose became furious and remarked that I didn't need to cause such a scene.

Rika said to my mother, "Aunt Reena, I cautioned not to bring this clumsy girl with you to the places like this," as Arta was so quiet and staring at me.

I noticed Ms. Elsa approaching toward us with another middle-aged woman then she asked, "Dear Ariana, what happened, what had my nephew done wrong that you had punished him in front of my visitors?"

"You didn't have any right to slap my son, do you know who he is?" the other woman who was with Ms. Elsa stated. "This is the outcome of opening the gate to low class individuals, I had advised Elsa pick her guests from well-known people or at the very least the one who could have a suitable dress for one night. Go apologize in front of everyone, please."

"Please ask your daughter to go and apologize right away," Ms. Elsa replied, turning to my mother.

They both departed after that, Mother, who had been crying, said to me, "See how much you have make me feel guilty in front of them, did you hear what she called us poor class? They wouldn't have humiliated us like this in front of all if you had just used your brain."

"Why are people fighting with Ariana and not Jack for what he asked?" questioned Arta.

"It was only an offer," Rika retorted, "Ariana has called everyone's reputation into doubt!"

Mother warned that if we didn't go and finish the apology, the entire town would be talking about us for the rest of our lives.

When I entered the women's restroom, Arta assisted me in getting ready before asking me to follow all her instructions.

I started to walk to his table and wished I had never entered that house. My hands were trembling, I couldn't keep my head up, and I felt as though my body had grown too heavy for my legs to support.

I could tell he was anxiously awaiting me because he was grinning. Before I could say anything, he spoke and said, "There's no need to apologize; I understand you're a beginner. Unfortunately, tonight wasn't my lucky night. Have a great evening."

We were waiting for Rose and Rika to arrive as the guests left one after the other, but shockingly both were missing this time!

"I hope all of you will erase what occurred tonight and go home with good hearts, especially you, Ariana," Ms. Elsa said as she and her husband waited at our table. "Edwin didn't get a chance to spend time with you tonight, so I love you two to know each other more."

Mom was extremely happy when she said, "We'll be there for sure; it's our joy to be a part of Mr. Edwin's great day."

When Rika and her mother finally appeared, they were prepared to depart.

Everyone spoke well of the party on the way, but not me because I was too exhausted and concerned about my upcoming mathematics test.

It was after one in the morning.

After I removed my cursed clothing, my mother instructed me to clean the kitchen. When I arrived to object, I noticed her upset expression and simply replied, "Sure."

Chapter 4
Sepia

When our allotted time had passed and the math teacher was gathering the test papers, he asked me, "Ms. Baker, what is this?" Even though I hadn't answered a single question.

He said he would report this to the principal, and I had nothing to say in response.

What could I possibly tell him. Which one was appropriate that I was attending Ms. Elsa's birthday party and didn't have time or too busy cleaning the house and washing the dishes till three in the morning? Even if he tells my family about this, as if they would care!

When it was time for a break, I didn't want to leave the house; instead, I wanted to lay down at my desk and sleep something that I desperately needed.

After my nap, I felt much better, so I told Catherine not to worry. She then indicated that our principal was calling for me, and I ignored her.

She stood behind her desk, holding my papers in her hand, so I knew what it was about.

"There are just two months left, Ariana. Why aren't you fighting?" She signaled for me to sit. "Why did you quit? I understand your history and that you need this, but I had higher expectations."

I broke down in tears and told her what happened last night. She stated that, sadly, my mother has restarted and that, because she did the same thing with Arta as well, it indicates that she isn't willing to give up.

She advised me to be brave and try to continue with my studies no matter what since they are the only thing that will one day save me after I told her about what was occurring in the house.

Ms. Jane (the principal) requested from the math teacher that I be given the exam once more after school.

Mother and Ms. Jane were classmates, and I recall my mother telling me about how, when she was just as young, her family pressured her into marriage. I suppose this made her luckier than other women, because her husband would eventually pass away from some form of cancer.

She will then be referred to as a 'curst woman', and people will avoid wanting to interact with her. Her only option is to finish her studies; since her spouse passed away, and not even her family has gone to get her. She was being ignored by everyone because they believed her bad luck would spread! She eventually found her way and was made the principal of the school where all the girls in the town sent there to study!

I was confident that my mother would inform me that I had fallen under Ms. Jane's spell if she discovered that I had been in her office. Mom urged me to go downstairs and check on Grandmother when I got home after my exam and witnessed my mother and father arguing.

I was overjoyed, immediately changed, grabbed my text book, and left. Grandma had a cold and was not feeling well. She was delighted to see me and hurried into the kitchen to begin preparing some soup.

I sat in the kitchen to work on my assignments because it was so quiet and I also served myself a bowl of soap. Grandma had instructed me to wake her after I finished reviewing everything, but it took me almost two hours.

When I left her house and entered ours, I could still hear my parents arguing. I don't know what had happened to them so suddenly; they typically only battled for five minutes before stopping.

When I explained to Arta why I had to go to her place this time, she requested me to keep quiet because Analia had just fallen asleep. Without noticing me, her husband Benjamin was watching television when he said, "Oh it's you, why are you clutching your books afterwards?"

Arta requested that she accompany her to the kitchen because it was in such a dreadful shape and she had no chance to finish her work there because of Analia. She said that she had gone to see Benjamin's cousin, who had traveled from Sweden, and that she had been driven insane by the way she was dressed and the jewelry she was sporting. She briefly hopes she could put herself in her position.

Following that, she began to inquire as to why our parents were at odds. I answered her, "Mother was yelling at father to explain why he quit honoring her anniversaries, why she doesn't have money to buy good clothes, or why they no longer interact as a pair. Because Dad works full-time at the bakery, he is never at home, and at the end of the day, he just comes and sleeps."

Arta said, "Mom was right, she never had any anniversaries."

Because he believes that women should only be used for domestic tasks like cooking, cleaning, and child care, Dad, an old-fashioned man, has abandoned Mom.

She also claimed that Dad's ideas had infected Benjamin and that he was becoming more and more like our father, but she wouldn't allow him to harm her. Instead, she cited Aunt Rose as having a very understanding husband who makes her and her family extremely happy. But as you can see, none of us are content.

I excused myself and went because I didn't want to be a part of this conversation. When I returned, the door was open, and Adam was dressed for a night out with his friends. Father was reading newspaper, and Mom was in the kitchen.

I left the book in my room and walked to the kitchen. When Mother asked me why I was leaving the house, I replied that it was she who had instructed me to leave.

I had only thought of spaghetti when she asked me to make something for dinner, so I got to work right away.

At the dinner, my parents were not even looking at each other. My mother was trying to aggravate my father by telling me that it would be best if I stayed with my grandma since she was ill and needed company.

My father replied that the elderly woman needed a nurse and had the ability to hire one, so his daughter was not needed to go there, and although I thought the concept was wonderful, I refrained from saying anything.

"Don't forget you are living in her house, so be grateful. If she kicks our stuff out, can you get us elsewhere with your income," Mom snapped back at him.

He didn't respond and walked to the room after finishing his dinner. While scrubbing the table, Mother was muttering to herself, "I need to phone Rose and ask her when is the actual date for Ms. Elsa's son birthday, and get the number of their tailor, the one who sewed Rika and Rose clothes, this time I won't allow anybody to take us down, I will teach them."

I went to visit my grandmother after packing a few clothes and taking my school bag.

I was still content when she told me that she didn't have a bed ready for me, but that I could sleep on the sofa tonight.

I remember being awakened at around four in the morning by the sound of my grandma reciting aloud from one of her old poetry volumes. I could tell she was inattentive to me as she continued. She asked me what was wrong after I got up and walked to the library room.

I assured her that I would sit down and study for the exam. I believe it was a wise decision; every night, I read aloud to Grandma. We returned to our own rooms and fell asleep after an hour. I was stress-free and enjoying my time.

Chapter 5
Tropical Rain Forest

I was curious about how my mother acquired the funds for the clothing she had bought for me, and I later learned that she had sold the silver jewelry set Grandmother had given her.

Arta was compelled to order a new nightgown as well, and she eventually secured Benjamin's blessing and the necessary funds. Rose and Rika got along quite perfectly and never had any issues purchasing dresses of any kind.

I'm not sure why, but after I put on the dress, I felt happy, and I started seeing myself dancing on stage with Edwin. I'm not sure what caused me to start feeling this way about him. Despite being weird, it was pleasant. I kept asking, "Is this what I want?" And kept trying to come up with an answer.

Mom was so sure I would win his love and he wouldn't stop pursuing me.

The finest thing that ever occurred to me was staying with Granma, and as a result, I was able to pass nearly all of my tests with high marks. When Granma discovered about the whole event, she yelled, "Your mother was not pleased with her marriage from the start, selling her set and buying an outfit, is ridiculous, she doesn't have money, why she is trying to join these kinds of parties, all is Rose's mistake, she is the one who has begun all these disasters."

She was correct, and I was aware of it, but I refrained from responding since I felt compelled to attend the party and didn't want to stop it.

I was delighted to have my own room with a bed and wardrobe after Grandma gave it to me. That evening, we had dinner together before I completed my studies and went to bed. That evening, I had trouble falling asleep.

The following day at school, Catherine was asking more questions than I could handle since she was so eager. When I went home, I saw that the hallway had undergone some adjustments.

What occurred when I was in school, I questioned my mother. She replied, laughing, "There were some useless items in the house that weren't being utilized, so I decided to sell them, like your father's guitar, Adam's video games and his television, as well as a few of the portraits. Insisted I have bought the diamond earrings for you, though, as they really go with your dress!"

She had sold our household belongings to buy me a diamond earring, which I couldn't believe. She instructed me to join her squad and defend her and her beliefs as I held my chest and sat on the kitchen chair.

"Does Daddy know about this," I questioned?

She yelled at me, "Why should I ask his permission when he has already declared that he won't meddle with anything and doesn't care?"

We had all been preparing for this day, and when it finally arrived, I was gorgeous in my dress and diamond earrings. When Arta said that she had never had the chance to showcase her beauty, Mother responded, "You weren't gentle, the first guy who grinned at you; you fell in love and married him, but this time I want to show the whole city, what I am capable of."

I suppose this was a struggle for Mother, who was determined to triumph at all costs, but Arta's account was entirely different from what Mother claimed. I recall Rika accompanying her, and the two of them competing to find the best husbands—best in their eyes, meaning the richest.

Mother wanted Arta to date Benjamin because his parents work in the freight industry and she also planned to push him to get engaged to her. Following their brief marriage, his parents decided to sell all of their possessions, turn everything into cash, and retire. Mother's estimations were incorrect in this area.

Due to the fact that Benjamin didn't have a job or any money and that their lives were dependent on his commissions from the super market he started working for, he eventually asked my dad for a place to live, and they were able to rent the third floor of my grandmother's home.

While we awaited Rose and Rika to pick us up, we were all dressed up. Rika was really upset to see me arrive, and her clothing resembled Arta's.

Aunt had on so much makeup that I hardly saw her eyes. I didn't mind when Rika told me that I had finally learned how to choose right clothes. Rika informed her mother that she would be driving, and so they switched places.

Like before, the celebration was held in their home, but this time, all of the seating and decorations were new and far more sophisticated.

There were both young boys and girls, and Ms. Elsa was the one who came to welcome us in. "Edwin invited all of his college pals, so it seems like we're the elderly people at this party," she remarked.

"I wish you had forgotten what occurred the last time and tried to cheer up and be livelier on the dance platform this time, since you are prettier than what I could anticipate," she remarked as she turned to face me.

As she led us to our seats, I frantically searching for Edwin. Rika was so upset that Harold was not invited, and Rose just took off once she saw Mr. Jack on the dance stage.

We were just sitting there as Arta began to eat from the appetizer plates that were placed on our table; I don't see why they were called appetizers because they were virtually desserts. Mom urged her to restrain herself and save some room for dinner.

My mother had already advised me not to ruin my makeup, so I was unable to eat anything.

Zack stepped over and shook my hand without paying attention to the other diners at the table.

I wish this party was my party and I could be the one who gets the first dance. "Can't believe you are the same person, who I met last time, so gorgeous." It drew his comment.

While Arta sat with her mouth full, Mother pretended to be watching the dancing stage. I was waiting for someone to protect me from him. I saw Ms. Elsa approached and ask my mother whether it was alright for her to take me along?

"What belongs to me belongs to you," Mother responded. I gave in and went with her once more. Zack made me feel somewhat uncomfortable to continue on, but once I realized where she was leading me, I became anxious. I had been waiting to meet Edwin all this time, but now I didn't want to even look at him. Being rejected once more terrified me.

This time, he stepped up to greet me and welcome me, and after I formally congratulated him on his birthday, birthday, I debated whether to stay or go because I didn't want the same incident to happen again.

I don't know why, but I felt like my hand was burning in his when he was holding it as he led me to his special place.

He remarked, looking at me and asking, "What do I think?"

"I had urged my mother not to invite too many people but, she won't listen, I always like modest parties, or simply celebrations with loved ones."

I agreed with him as well, and as he began to discuss Paris and his life there, I was ecstatic to hear him speak. He appeared so endearing! His eyes were enchanted, and his cherry-colored lips were whispering the love words as he spoke. I was falling under his spell.

He spoke briefly, and when the meal was served, I noticed that my mother was still grinning and radiating satisfaction.

Ms. Elsa asked me if I would like to join my family while we sat at the dinner table, but Edwin objected. I couldn't believe he wouldn't let me leave, even for a moment, to be with my family. "Mom, she's fine here," he said.

He served me first, followed by himself. After we started eating, I saw Zack was staring at us. I was unable to finish my meal after seeing his disappointed face, so I excused myself to leave. Edwin grabbed my arm and said he was also finished.

He explained to me what his cousin did the last time was wrong and that he had incorrectly evaluated.

When I explained that I was being held accountable for what I had done and had been forced to apologize, he continued to stand by me and stated, "You, apologizing doesn't change the full story, you defended yourself and I appreciated that."

I was overjoyed because he was so kind and could see how I ended up doing it.

"I am so delighted to start a relationship with a girl like you and started having a wonderful feeling about us; I didn't have any meaningful relationships before save for one," he said, asking the bartender to pour us two glasses of his unique cocktail. "She was a French girl, and although our romance was brief, she passed away from cancer. I was hesitant to begin a new relationship after her until I met you. Is it your desire to be my girlfriend?"

It would have been appropriate for me to have responded at this point with: "This is my pleasure to be at your side as your GIRL," but I was happy he had picked me out from among all the other girls there.

He invited me to dance with him, but I had trouble understanding the French language music so we were both staring into each other's eyes. I was also daydreaming the entire time.

After the music has stopped, everyone applauded as we returned to our special seat like a queen and her king. He spoke as he gripped my hand and kept it close to his heart. It usually doesn't beat too quickly, therefore I assume it is aware of tonight's events. He added, "Thank you for selecting me; I won't let you regret." And I felt shy.

Zack's request for Edwin to take the stage to accept his gift from his parents worried us.

"Is it okay if I take you to your family so they can make sure you won't be bothered before I leave?" he asked.

I replied, "Absolutely."

He told me he wouldn't be shocked if he didn't see Rose and Rika among the guests as we walked together to where Arta his mother were sitting.

What am I to say? He was correct; perhaps it was best for him to be fully informed before deciding to become a member of our family!

Mom, who started greeting Edwin and complimenting him on the entertainment for the evening and, let's not forget, wishing him nearly six times, couldn't conceal her joy.

"I didn't know you are this good at attracting the most desired boy in town," Arta said as she sat down next to me after Edwin apologized and departed.

Mother expressed her admiration for me and asked, "Now tell me, which one is better, studying or enjoying your life with Edwin?"

I once did something that made everyone happy of me, I thought, but I kept it to myself, that it was evident that spending time with Edwin was more enjoyable than sitting and reading the same book repeatedly.

Edwin received numerous gifts, and each one cost more than my father's lifesavings!

He asked me to accompany him after cutting his cake and bringing my portion with him. This time, as we sat on the luxurious seats by the pool, he declared that I was the best gift he could have ever received.

I never considered myself to be a gift for someone's birthday!

He added that if I don't mind, he can ask all the questions he has about me in his head. I gave him free rein to ask me everything he wanted, including whether I have a father, where I reside, and what my family's occupation is.

I was certain he wanted to get to know me better because he asked me so many personal questions, and I didn't tell any lies.

"I enjoy going to school; it's my desire to become a lawyer," I remarked. Going to college is a good thing, but you shouldn't devote all of your time to it. There are other significant events in life that are worth celebrating and enjoying, especially with loved ones.

Oh my goodness, he had it all—he was attractive, endearing, empathetic, intelligent, wealthy, lovable, and came from a wonderful family. This is the stuff of every girl's fantasy! I had that thought. I was fortunate, and that was only possible due of my understanding and devoted Mother!

Then he said he is a brilliant violinist and he would love to play for me tonight after asking me if I knew how to play any music and that I had previously answered this question for his cousin as well.

There was still music playing inside; I assume the helpers had already told the band to stop when he gave the order for the violin to be brought to him.

I had no experience playing music, but the manner he was playing and the motion of his hand were incredible. I was on the verge of tears as he played some extraordinarily moving but extremely sad songs.

I didn't notice when everyone came out until we heard them clapping after he finished performing!

I don't know why, but I felt like I needed a little space, so I hurriedly excused myself and walked to the ladies' restroom. I was tense and terrified of what was beginning inside of me. I had to leave.

It was just not the perfect time to let him know that I was falling in love with him because that was my weakness. I was having trouble breathing, and my hands were shaking. I could have wed him tonight even if I wasn't ready to do so.

She then shut the door and went into the same bathroom where I was hiding, shut the door, and said, "What is wrong with you, once I thought you were all OK, acting like a grown up, now you are in here weeping? You continue to be the idiot." She added, "He is our final chance; if you lose him, you have lost us as well. If there are no more dreams of going to or completing school, she remarked as harshly as she could, refreshed my makeup, and replaced my lipstick."

"I'll allow you to endure pain for the rest of your life," Mom said.

What could I have said? After forgetting entirely why I was crying, I finally regained my calmness.

When we had both exited the restroom, Edwin approached me and asked, "Are you alright, did I do anything wrong? Has Jack bothered you once again?"

I answered him. "No, the music was so beautiful that it made me cry; I couldn't believe someone could play the violin that well."

He wasn't satisfied with my response, but I suppose it was good enough at the time.

When it was time for us to depart, Ms. Elsa called him to come and escort the guests.

Arta made the decision to seize the wheel because Rose and Rika were wasted as usual.

When we all said farewell, Edwin was still gazing at me and grinning sweetly. He said he had already begun arranging for his upcoming visit because he couldn't wait.

Mother requested her sister and niece come spend the night at our house while everyone else was quiet on the road.

I went to Grandmother while she slept, went to the bathroom, and while wearing all of my clothing, stood under the shower, thinking about Edwin. My mother was correct; I am a dumb girl.

I was unable to sleep, and although I had school the next day, I hardly remembered what I was meant to accomplish! Everything I was thinking about was him and him alone.

What a night it was!

Chapter 6
Mano Tango

First term results were announced. Although I was the first in the class, there was still a long way to go as this was only one term.

Instead of rejoicing, I began to stress over my year-end reports. Sicilia placed second in the class and was unhappy; I don't know why, but I felt bad for her. Perhaps college was for her and not for me. My principal was overjoyed and she was the one holding the papers in her hands.

I hadn't heard from Edwin since that evening. He might have changed his mind and selected someone else, or he might have discovered that my family wasn't a suitable fit for his.

Unfortunately, I was unable to visit him or call him since my mother warned us to maintain our calmness because he would undoubtedly come searching for me.

I was constantly thinking about holding Edwin's hand and dancing with him. I had lost awareness of my actions and all I wanted was Edwin. Once in the school, suddenly heard Catherine yelling, and I could see Ms. Jane too, but why were they rushing up to me?

Yes, I did pass out in the school. I opened my eyes to discover that I was in a hospital. Mother was arguing with Ms. Jane in front of the doctor when she was present. "My daughter was okay when she left the home this morning, for sure the principal had done some magic on her and cursed her or given her a one of her portions," she was adding.

I had lost all strength, no one knew I was in love, and the only thing I wanted was him. How could my mother have missed it and been blaming Ms. Jane?

I later received a visit from Ms. Jane, who wished me a speedy recovery and said, "Ariana, I don't know what is wrong with you, but I am quite certain that it has something to do with your mother and her ambitions. We are living in a tiny town, so word will spread quickly. I heard you were away for Ms. Elsa's son's birthday, and although you two have grown rather close, this is not the time or even the appropriate age for you! Give yourself another year and see if you don't think differently about things."

Before I could speak, my mother entered and gestured for her to leave. Mom questioned me, "What was the witch asking you? Was she attempting to brainwash you once more?"

The nurse contacted my mother and instructed her to meet the doctor in the waiting room as I was shaking and not yet stable. I simply buried myself in a blanket and burst into tears.

My father and the doctor, it appears, had a meeting planned, and the principal was also included.

I tried to relax as the nurse asked, "Is there anything you need to share with us?" I said 'no' by shaking my head.

She then gave me another injection, which put me to sleep and caused me to lose all memory of that day.

The following morning when I awoke, I discovered that Arta had entered the room with a hand full of chocolates while my mother was absent. She claimed that it was stored in the lobby for no charge! She added that the doctor wanted me to heal fully and would keep me for another day or two. When I inquired about my mother, I was informed that she had returned home to rest.

I was dying to hear what she had to say when she said, "Mother is planning to invite Edwin and his family, but she has reserved the beach house restaurant. Can you believe, we will finally see that restaurant we have always wanted to see?"

I shouted and exclaimed, "Are you serious?" I believe she also sensed the changes occurring inside of me. We both cheered.

She assumed I was just as eager to see the beach house as she was, but in my head, I was sitting next to Edwin, holding hands, and arranging our future together!

Mother didn't share with me what the doctor told them in front of the principal that day. To expeditiously be released from the hospital, I started to eat whatever food they had given me and tried to walk and balance on my own.

This time, it was my concern over what to dress around Edwin and his family.

Chapter 7
Yellow Green

The celebration was going to be at the beach house restaurant, and Mom and Dad were always arguing about it. It appears like Mom did everything without telling Dad, and when she ran out of money, she told him and pleaded for help. She claimed that he would never have offered his assistance if she had told him.

*Since **I** missed school and my classmates during my five-day sick absence, everyone was glad to see me return.*

When the phone rang that day after I had returned home, my mother wanted me to answer it. I was shocked because she never allows me to do so because she thinks I have a bad sense of communication.

"Greetings, I'm really sorry; I was unaware that you had been admitted to the hospital."

I was about to scream when I realized it was him, and my mother was still laughing.

When it was my turn to speak, I froze. When my mother walked over to me and hard-pinned my arm, I yelled, "Hi, I was stressed after my tests, I think I lost so much energy, but now I am good, thanks for asking."

"I have already spoken with your mother, and she has given me permission to come and pick you up today. I can't wait to meet you," he said. "Bye, my Cinderella, be ready at five."

I was still holding the phone and remained paralyzed once more since I had no time to react.

Mother urged me to wash and get ready right away because it appeared like there was a lot to do.

I tried on several of Arta's clothing as my mother got to work on my hair and makeup. I was thinking that although though I had a report on our science experiment that I needed to write and turn in the next day, Edwin was right that I needed to spend some time with him. "Edwin is a tressure; if you can win his love and force him to marry you, we will all profit from this marriage, including your father and Adam," she said, trying to provide a justification for leaving my comfort zone. "You need to attempt to be careful; don't give him whatever he requests; instead, let him always be hungry. Only on the wedding night will you succeed."

While getting dressed, Mother grabbed my hand and said, "Don't blow this chance. We're all depending on you. Try to invite him personally to the beach house party."

He was there in the brand-new automobile that his folks had given him for his birthday. After a brief moment of staring at each other in the car as he inquired, "Where do you plan to go?" When I informed him I didn't have a specific location in mind, he suggested that we head to his place instead.

He inquired about my hospital admission, and when I decided to be forthright from the start, I replied, "Someone grabbed my heart; it was too tough to maintain a body without a heart."

He grinned, pulled my hand closer to his chest, and he began driving the car.

We arrived at an old farm that was distant from my house. He was able to park his car inside, and he explained that this had been their family home for the previous four generations. When their parents decide to move to Paris, they will just leave the house in its current condition.

I was hesitant to descend since I felt a little afraid and I was wondering why he had brought me here rather than someplace more enjoyable.

He led me to the second story, where there was a lovely fireplace and sofas gathered around it despite the fact that the yard was completely neglected and the building was enormous.

There wasn't much to do, and it was filthy and dusty. I wasn't dressed for this.

I approached him and sat down next to him on the sofa as he opened his arm. He pulled me even closer to him and held me there while yelling, "I am falling in LOVE with you, no one else can possess you."

I observed his eyes and assumed that he was not lying.

The only items in the kitchen, aside from some tea bags and a kettle, were when he went there to look for something to eat. I agree when he offered me a cup of tea.

Despite the fact that I was quite hungry and it was getting dark, I should have been home by now, he insisted that I have supper with him in the unsettling house.

I respectfully declined his offer and requested him to drive me home before it got too late; nevertheless, he didn't like it and said, "I want to remain the night here and I want you to stay with me, don't you trust me?"

I sat down next to him and said, "Please don't do this. We have just started our friendship, my father doesn't know I am with you, and if he finds out, he will never let us meet again." I was honestly not prepared for this sort of behavior from him at the time.

"Only under one condition will I let you go; you must guarantee that I can see you whenever I want, without any limitations, and that I also require directions to your school."

I gave him my word and any information he required regarding the school since I was happy that he desired me so very much. Was there anyone else in my life before him, he asked me in front of our building. I informed him, "I have told you; I am not in a relationship; my concentration is on my education."

I was feeling shy and worried that someone might have seen us when he pulled me forward and kissed me. He asked me not to tell anyone where we had been.

"Where have you gone, your father wanted to come home two hours ago, and I have made up a fictitious shopping list and sent him to the market." Mother was sitting in the kitchen, looking so worried. "Tell me where you were, whether you were acting appropriately, and where he took you."

I lied to my mother and said, "He was taking me to the beautiful coffee shop, he was talking and expressing his feeling for me and planned for our future, I couldn't stop him, it was extremely disrespectful," because I had to safeguard my friendship and be faithful to my lover and future husband.

"Did you invite him to the beach house dinner?" my mother inquired as her expression changed and a smile broke through. I assured her that I had entirely forgotten. She made one of her normal sweet remarks to me, saying, "You are so foolish, how come this boy is falling in love with you."

I dressed quickly and headed downstairs since she wanted me to visit my grandparents before Dad got home. Grandma yelled at me for visiting her so late and was as grumpy as ever. I absolutely neglected to take off my makeup, but as soon as she saw me, she felt awful for me and let me in.

"I have one task before I pass away."

She gave her a face kiss and remarked, "I didn't understand what she meant."

Grandma called me when she overheard me talking to myself and said, "I have to do some reading before I fall asleep. Can you join me? I don't want to be alone. You may bring your books and read in the hallway, like this both can advantage."

She was fantastic because I was able to finish my science report while sitting by her side.

She would sometimes make an effort to stay up late, however she did it for me because she wanted me to focus on my schoolwork and other projects. I assume the mission she was referring to was my academic career.

I told Catherine everything about Edwin and I the following day. I had managed to keep Edwin out of the school for a few hours in my head. I planned to take the bus home, saw Edwin was waiting for me next to the bus stop.

"It seemed I couldn't wait for so long, are you hungry?" He then got down and opened a door for me in a gentlemanly manner; I couldn't believe he was there. I shook his hand and informed him that I was indeed hungry now that I had seen him.

After that, we went to a classy restaurant for a wonderful lunch, and this time I remembered to invite him!

Chapter 8
Timber Wolf

I had a wonderful dress ready for our party, but I was not in the mood to even try it on.

Mother forbade me from calling Edwin since he hadn't called or shown up to pick me up. He used to pick me up every day, take me out to lunch, and then drive me home, so it was too evident that I was really in love with him.

Mother was invited by her sister to the party which was tomorrow. We were unable to invite anyone else because the venue was so pricey. Grandmother was not at all pleased to see us; she claimed it was premature to start thinking about marriage. However, I believe she spoke a little too late; at the time, all I wanted was to be with Edwin.

Rarely would Dad close the bakery, but that day, after a heated argument with Mom, he ultimately made the decision to do so that evening. Adam and Dad each received a suit, and it was the first time we saw our father dressed appropriately, well shaven.

Poor mother, I used to feel so bad for her. Why couldn't Daddy be more understanding and try to help out every so often? I was wondering that perhaps if he had spent a bit more time with his wife, their troubles would have been far less.

Before the guests arrived, we came a little early to make sure everything was in order. A VIP table was provided for us, and it had the best view of the orchestra and the sea.

Even though Rose and her family arrived early, Edwin had yet to communicate. "I didn't realize you are that good at trap his heart, keep it up," my aunty urged as she arrived to congratulate me.

Ariana is too young to realize what is best for her, she is a foolish kid, and she cannot read signs, stated Rika in response to her Mother's remark, which made her unhappy.

There are no other signals save the symbols of LOVE and marriage, so what are you talking about, Arta snapped huffily? "Have you ever thought, why a boy in his level should fall in love with a girl in her level?" she asked, lowering her voice slightly so that her father wouldn't hear. "After achieving his goal, he won't even remember her name because you have what he really desired."

Mother assured her, "Ariana is stronger than you can think." And she is making sure to supervise all of my movements. Since I was so concerned that Edwin wouldn't show up, I honestly did not care what they were discussing!

After a while, I noticed his car and immediately wanted to go outside, but my mother stopped me and told me that I should behave like a mature girl because my father is also present. Mom was right; I needed to contain myself as Rika laughed so loudly at my excitement.

Edwin, who is so lovely and elegant and was carrying a large arrangement of flowers, followed Ms. Elsa as she went while wearing a gorgeous outfit and holding her husband's hand.

All of us stood up in front of them, with Mother taking the lead in introducing us and directing them to their seats. Except for Dad, who was merely appearing to smile and was otherwise absent, everyone appeared to be joyful. Mr. Neal, Aunt Rose's husband, was, as always, hilarious.

I was asked to join Edwin for a dance after dinner when the band started playing some good music. I looked at my mother, who gave the go-ahead by shaking her head.

There was only the two of us on the dance floor, and I couldn't stop staring at my father, which was extremely uncomfortable. The moment I saw Arta walking onto the platform holding Benjamin's hand and Rose and Neal getting up from their seats to join us, I believe Arta and Mother had caught on.

I was relieved, when I asked Edwin why he wasn't picking me up anymore, he said that he was out playing football with his friends and couldn't make it. On the other days, he was working with his father. He said, "I was missing you so much and wanted to come to you, but I was afraid of your father. How are you, sweetheart? Just thinking about you makes me feel alive every day." I would have been the one to kiss him this time if my father hadn't been present.

After we had danced together, he led me to my seat. There, in front of everyone, he pulled a silver box from his pocket, opened it, and kept the contents on my table a **diamond necklace**!

He said, "We didn't need to hide our love from anyone," so my mother started cheering, and everyone else joined her. My father was still dissatisfied, but I didn't care about that longer.

Except for Dad, who appeared to have had no other option, everyone had a good time that evening. "Ariana, tonight you proved to me you deserved to be treated like Royals," Mother began singing and clapping the car.

Following that day, my mother started letting us see each other more frequently. We went to a few parties and dance clubs, and he represented me to everyone as his girlfriend! However, I didn't want to frighten him; I loved being his fiancée.

One of those parties had an unusual incident occur. We were invited to a pool party, and everyone was wearing swimsuits, except for me. Edwin wouldn't let me wear a swimsuit, and I didn't want to either.

All were wasted during the pool party, and since I was so exhausted, I decided to take a stroll around the villa. I was out alone when a lad approached and asked if he could hang out with me. I told him I was waiting for Edwin, but he insisted.

Since no one could stop Edwin from hitting the man after he spotted him there near me, the poor man's face was covered in blood. I begged him to stop, but he continued until he ran out of breath.

I tried to talk to him to calm him down as we hurriedly approached the car, but he yelled at me, "I've told you a million times that you only belong to me, and no one can take you."

He yelled at me harsher this time and said, "Keep your mouth close or I'll tear you to pieces," as I attempted to explain.

Chapter 9
Vivid Violet

In less than two weeks were the final exams, and I was really struggling this time because it was difficult to balance being a student and a girlfriend. We received a vacation from class to prepare for finals.

Catherine began her lecture by asking, "Ariana if your boyfriend would let you study this time because, You are being pursued by Sicilia; one mistake will mean game over."

She was correct; Sicilia did not waste any time and continued to study during school breaks. But what about me? I've gone on twenty birthday celebrations, twelve nightclubs, ten concerts, and a ton of lunch and dinner get-togethers with Edwin's pals since we initially met.

"Ariana, why won't he let you come over to my house anymore?" Catherine asked. "Why is it that you are only allowed to be with him and not with any of your friends or family members?"

For the first time, I desired for her to speak with me and serve as a constant reminder of my identity and my development.

"Ariana, I fear him, last time he picked you up from school, he threw his coffee cup at me, even though my uniform was dirty! Why would he be so angry with me when he doesn't even know me?"

My mother was my biggest nightmare because I had no answers for her queries, didn't even know what I wanted anymore, was behaving as his doll and walked everywhere with him.

She hugged me back and said, "No matter what, you are my best friend, and nothing can change that, not even Edwin."

To which I replied, "Please give me some time; I will become myself very soon."

Everyone at school observed the changes I was going through, and they were anticipating that I would invite them to my wedding soon. Even my mother was nagging me to make him marry me, as we lived in a small town, and she was unable to hide the fact that people were talking about us any longer.

I was okay with not having him pick me up from school that day because I walked the entire way home while reflecting on my life. Instead of going up for change, I went straight to Grandmother.

Without saying a word, she opened the gate and let me in. I came inside and went to take a shower despite not being at all hungry. I was lying on my bed when Grandma entered the room and inquired, "What's happening, Ariana? Are you upset?"

As soon as I caught a glimpse of her eyes, I lost all self-control and started sobbing uncontrollably. My throat was being constricted, making it impossible for me to breathe. I confessed to her that I didn't feel well.

Edwin smacked me so hard the last time I was at his house in front of his mother that, if Ms. Elsa hadn't been present, I was certain he wouldn't stop. I was never able to discuss any of them with my family; the one time I did, my mother punished me and claimed that she was certain that I was the one who started the argument because, Edwin is a gentleman.

"Back then, women had certain rights and obligations; she was not permitted to visit her fiancé's home and remain up late. The engagement and subsequent wedding took place in a week or two after the girl and guy were only permitted to meet in front of their parents. I am aware that these things are absurd and pointless in your day, but the girl needed this form of protection because both her body and her emotions were difficult to access," Grandma said.

"Your mother was not permitted to do any of things, which she is pressuring you to do, since she didn't believe in luck and wanted to control everything herself, she was unhappy with her own marriage and wanted to see achievement in her children," she said as she began brushing my hair. "See what she has done to you, look at you! Are you the same Ariana who was searching for a quiet place to study her topic for school?"

What could I do, what was left for me to do while I was still crying, confused, and lost? I have to be with him since I don't have a future, my mom was admonishing.

"He has such a high opinion of himself; pampered rat! I stopped liking him. He doesn't have a goal in life and doesn't respect any of your family members, not even your dad or even me; everything he wants, he gets right away. Why don't you recognize that the way he treats us is wrong?" Grandmother said.

"Grandma, it's too late to stop it now because I didn't sign up for any of these," I responded.

"It's never too late to act morally." She grinned as she replied. "By assigning you a ton of work, I'll try to keep you occupied at home so you can begin your finals preparation. Additionally, you can make up an illness that requires rest so that we can allow you some time to concentrate on your actual future. In the meantime, you make an effort to let him know that you need to end your relationship with him and that I can also speak to your mother because you are no longer interested in it."

After learning about her plans, I was so relieved that Grandma was at least by my side.

Around ten o'clock that evening, Edwin arrived to fetch me up. Grandma had informed him that I wasn't feeling well, but he didn't want to go. I had to answer the phone when he kept calling at midnight because I didn't want Granny to wake up.

"You lied to me, as did your foolish grandmother. Now that you've rejected me, who the heck are you? I've already said that I need to see you anytime I want." Because I was terrified, I said, "She didn't lie to you, it's late, and I'm sleepy and little ill."

"Shut up, I'll pick you up tomorrow after school. Don't let me enter the premises and beat you in front of your pals."

Chapter 10
Black

I studied all night and didn't get any sleep before Edwin arrived early in the morning. I hugged Grandma, thanked her for her support, and apologized for not following her plans when she advised me to speak to Edwin and end this relationship as I was leaving.

"How much longer did you want to wait to get ready?" he said while fuming in the car.

I apologized for being late.

I had never saw him drive in such a reckless manner; I thought we could collide. We arrived at their old home, which was located outside of town, as usual. He jumped out of the car, pulled me outside. My face was burning as he continued to hit me; I begged him to stop, but he grew angry, grabbed my hair, and pushed me upstairs.

I warned him that he had no right to strike me. He shouted and said, "You and that old witch have united against me; she has been training you to neglect me, and I can see how much you have transformed."

Afterward, threw me on the couch and said, "Change into one of those nightgowns and wait for me till I return."

He exited the house and locked every window, door, and gate. There was, tragically, no way out. My lips were bleeding, I was in pain. Still in amazement that he had injured me!

I hurriedly changed, refreshed my makeup, put on his favorite color, came, and sat by the fireplace; however, that day I waited a very long time for him to return.

He was carrying two boxes of pizzas, a large quantity of alcoholic beverages, as well as some nuts and olives.

Since he appeared to be in good spirits and was smiling at me while holding out his arm, I went over to him and pressed my head against his shoulder while I questioned how he could have beaten me so severely.

My forehead was kissed, and he added, "It occurs in relationships, and it is really natural, some days are, full of love and kisses, and some are conflicts. This demonstrates how much I love you and care about you."

It was approximately eleven o'clock in the evening, and I really wanted to go home but was too afraid to ask. I tried to behave normally. We shared dinner together, and he snapped some shots of me as usual.

He finally came to a decision since he needed to drive tomorrow with his father to the city for a business meeting and he was exhausted.

He played a love song while we were driving and held my hand the entire time. After what I had seen of him earlier, I was no longer open to his trickery.

I was extremely careful not to wake Grandma because I was too exhausted to walk upstairs and change and didn't want them to see the scars on my face.

However, I noticed the kitchen light was on and went to see why it was on.

When I saw Grandma asleep on the floor with her face as white as snow and called out to her repeatedly but received no response, I swiftly fled upstairs, screamed for aid, and ran downstairs again.

My mother observed my face while my father and I were rushing and she became concerned for my safety. After telling them that Grandma needs assistance, I lost all memory and passed out.

The following morning, I believe I was awakened, and I saw my mother hiding her face and sobbing, while Arta was dressed in a black dress and attempting to serve tea to the guests.

When my mother noticed me leaving the bed and came to take my hand, she broke down in tears and said, "Grandma has passed away. Police are claiming it was not a natural death. She has been robbed, and she has been choked to death." I was still confused about what had happened.

I was still reeling from what had happened and trying to process it when Arta and a police officer entered. He asked me to accompany him to the police station so that I could answer some questions.

Mom joined me as well, but she left Aunt Rika in charge. We were immediately escorted to the Investigation room after arriving. The officer in charge was a female, and she began by getting my name and my connection to the victim. "Why were you late that night?"

"I was out with my fiancé, and as usual, we were strolling through the park and didn't even notice the passing of time," I responded.

"What has happened to your face?" the lady said as my mother fixed her attention on me. I had no idea what to say because I had not anticipated this.

"I had played basketball, and I believe this had occurred when I was warming up and having fun." I was lying to her nonstop!

"So, you left very early in the morning and walked in the park with your fiancé till late at night? Could you please put your fiancé's information on this piece of paper for me?"

I could have easily asked for assistance and told them about Edwin and how he was treating me, but I wasn't certain it was the best course of action.

The officer requested that I ask Edwin to pay them a visit, and I give them my word that he will. I was just considering who may harm an elderly woman in this way as I was traveling.

When I returned home, I had a fever and wanted to visit my grandmother, but the police had closed the door. I asked the officers to pass me my school bag and uniform, and one of them let me enter and pack my belongings.

I came across Grandma's poem book while packing, the one that she liked to read in the middle of the night. I picked it up, opened a page that she had already folded, and noticed that it was written in her handwriting.

"I just have one purpose in life: Please, God, help me preserve Ariana and her future."

Grandma, you dear thing. I couldn't stop crying.

Chapter 11
Scarlet

I spent a week at the house since the police forbade my father and I from leaving, so I took advantage of the opportunity to study as hard as I could for my finals. I was overjoyed that I was exempt from dressing up and going to any parties or clubs with Edwin.

Our phone calls were also being monitored, so I was using that as an excuse when he called me on the landline and, the majority of the time, my father was the one who answered.

We were finally given permission to leave the house, but the murderer had still not provided a statement! Rika had plans to take over the Grandmother's home and convert it into her workplace while Rose and her family were there virtually every day. Dad had no choice but to work extra hours in the bakery to make ends meet since they were always eating at our house.

When Arta called me in one morning as I was constructing my chemical journal on our balcony, she informed me that Edwin was present and that she had asked him to my room. I yelled at her in a fit of rage and demanded to know why she done that without consulting me.

"He has brought so many gifts with him for all of us, including candy, flowers, and even a bicycle for Analia, so now is the greatest moment to get over it," Arta said.

I yelled at her because I was furious that she had let him in without consulting me even though I knew that once he was inside, he would somehow manage to take me out with him.

He was lying on my bed as I entered the room, his shoes still on.

"I can't believe it, we weren't permitted to see each other for so many days," he stated. "Thankfully, Ms. Reena kept updating me every day about you, till yesterday, she informed me that I am allowed to come and take you with me to my friend's party."

I avoided his gaze by glancing out the window and said, "My grandmother was killed, and I was the one who found her body. I am still having nightmares and am having trouble falling asleep, so sadly I am not in the state to join you for any celebration!"

"Oh, shut up, she was too elderly and had already passed away; incidentally, the robber knocked her to the ground during the heist, so what? It implies that as a result of her passing, the entire planet should be frozen!"

I became irate and told him that because I was injured and weak and couldn't even join him for our previous secret get-togethers, he should give me some time to heal.

He yelled in my ear, "Don't let me go and tell your family, what have we been doing while we are together, you little loose skirt," after pushing me from the bed and hitting me so hard in the tummy that I was unable to breathe.

I was sobbing and attempting to hide beneath the bed so that anyone who entered wouldn't see me in that condition. He planned to wait for me in the car before heading there. Because I couldn't get dressed, I simply left the house with a black dress. They all saw me leave, but no one wanted to get involved. I wish someone had stopped me!

He made the decision to take me to their eerie home where we would share a meal and then rest before heading to the party. He purchased some marinated chicken for the barbecue on the way.

I had trouble eating anything! He always carried his camera around with him, and it was loaded with pictures of him wearing clothes and without.

After a time, he decided to take a nap and brought me into bed with him. I was unable to go asleep because my chest was still in pain.

I then remembered that Zack (Edwin's cousin) had told me something about Edwin at one of the parties, but I hadn't taken him seriously. I needed to be strong to stand in front of him and fight him back. I even teased him, telling him that he was attempting to make up anything to annoy me because he was feeling envious of our connection.

"Don't be so close to Edwin," he warned me, "because he is anxious and has some significant difficulties. Also, once he knows he is in love, he won't be afraid to pursue that love."

When the time came to go his friend's party, I asked him if it was okay to drop me off at home because I wasn't feeling well. He yanked my hair like a savage animal, and I felt like it was completely wrapped around his hand.

I left to get dressed instead of fighting. We arrived at his friend's apartment in the evening, where there was as usual a lot of alcohol, drugs, music, and dancing.

He was as wasted as before, I didn't consume any food or drink, I felt severe pain in my left side, and I knew something had happened to me when he hit me.

He arrived and asked me to dance with him. I wanted to refuse, but I was afraid he would harm me again, so I stepped up on stage and started dancing. I thought back to our first dance together and how strongly I wanted him—I would have given my life to spend just one minute with him!

I lost all control and, regrettably, puked in front of everyone. After a while, I pleaded with Edwin to take me to the hospital since I was unable to withstand the pain. He eventually brought me back to our seat and requested for assistance.

He warned me in the car that it would not be safe for him to take me to the hospital because staff would discover that he is drunken and would certainly do a quick investigation to confirm that it was him who had done it. He told me that after dropping me off at home, I can visit the hospital tomorrow.

I didn't care that he left me there alone since I was glad to be away from him.

When Aunt Rose and Rika arrived at our home after I got there and saw me wearing a dress and makeup, they immediately began to be ridiculous. "You couldn't wait for the funeral to be over before returning to your unlawful relationship with your partner," commented Rika.

Mother intervened and said, "Let her be. She had been ill for a while, and I was the one who requested Edwin to come and take her out. At least she might have some fresh air, it could assist her to change her mood."

I walked to my room and immediately went to bed without changing.

Grandma, I'll make sure to assist you with your mission before I nod off.

Chapter 12
Denim

I was able to attend for a checkup the very following day, and after an X-ray, I was informed that I had a cracked rib. I got some painkillers from them, and I was supposed to rest.

My mother was more concerned that Edwin wouldn't be able to accompany me because of my condition, and that he would wind up with another Candide than she was bothered about why this was happening to me.

When we came home, Mom called Edwin right once to let him know what had happened. Surprisingly, their housekeeper informed Mom that Ms. Elsa and her son had left the nation this morning for a month-long trip to Paris.

My mother was horrified to hear it, but I was as joyful as always and had no idea I was hurting! The best news ever was that I could heal completely and still continue studying.

I had my final exams very shortly, and I was confident that I could pass them all. I immediately thanked my grandma for keeping an eye on me since I knew in my heart that this had to do with her.

Father was at work, Adam was barely home, and Mother had lost control of him. Our home was eerily silent and quiet. Sadly, she entirely forgot about her own son because she was concentrating so much on Edwin and his family.

Only attending school when I had exams, I was happy with my grades and had gladly forgotten Edwin. However, there were times when I wondered how he could have avoided saying goodbye or even bringing up the topic of travel.

Mother had gotten so bothersome that she called their home every day to ask when they planned to return.

"This time," she said, "I need to make Edwin set aside the wedding day." We were simply friends, and nothing official was mentioned, but she refused to accept it.

This time, I felt really pleased about my scores. Finals were over, and I was eagerly awaiting the school's announcement.

Mother was stating that since I'm getting married soon, Edwin will make the decision rather than my dad, but I didn't care any longer; I was going to do it regardless because it was what I wanted to do.

The fact that I was with Edwin changed everything, including the way my father was feeling about the whole university thing. He just wanted to stand in front of Mother, so he promised to sign my letter. Father had been pleading with her to let me go to the main city and try to be open to everything.

I was so overjoyed that there was no room left in my heart for Edwin. Then, one unusual day, something happened.

My mother asked me to go and see who was at the door. When I did, I saw two guys asking for my parents: one was dressed in a full suit and appeared to be much older; the other was younger but still well-dressed, tall, and holding sunglasses.

I merely enquired as to their identities and the reason behind their search for my parents.

"I'll explain everything once and for all, but in the meantime, I'm Mr. Servan, Mr. Farhad's attorney (he pointed at the younger guy). If it's possible, we would like to speak with your parents."

Since I needed to get permission, I requested them to stay. I then hurried upstairs and told my mother about them. Since Rika, Rose, and Arta were also at our house, she didn't mind letting them in.

Both walked in and sat down on the couch. Our typical mother asked me to make them tea because they didn't feel comfortable with all the women looking at them at once.

"I genuinely apologize for disturbing you ladies by showing up at your doorstep without prior notice, but there is a valid reason for that," Mr. Servan said.

After taking a sip of his tea, he added, "Twenty years ago, your father, Mr. Taylor, would sell my client's father, Mr. Clarks, the entire building that we are currently in.

"Your father needed money to pay off bank debts, but his friend was too nice to demand the building right now. Instead, he permitted him to keep the house until his wife (your mother) passed away and made a pledge to keep it a hidden for many years."

He said, "I came to know your mother, was brutally killed regrettably, and we are very sorry for the shock and grief, I had informed Mr. Clarks' son, since his father had passed away too, so all his belongings will be handed over to his only son, Mr. Farhad who is present with me." Mom and Aunt Rika's faces were so entertaining, as if they were watching horror flicks, with their mouth open.

Mother screamed, "This little child is going to take our property away from us!" while behaving agitatedly as if she did not comprehend what he had said.

"How can we be sure that all of this is real and that you people are not the ones who butchered our mother so that you could inherit her properties?" Rose continued. "I don't know who you are or what culture or background you come from, but I just wanted to inform you that this is my property. If you say one more thing against me, I'll ask my lawyer to file a complaint against all of you."

Then he left the house, and as the lawyer followed him, he said, "We will resolve this matter in court; if you have any questions or concerns, please feel free to bring them up or even apply your right to file a complaint against my client. Blessings," then shut the door.

Mother was so irate that she kept yelling rubbish at those men, and Rose was supporting her. "I don't see why you two are so heated, first of all, they need to have appropriate prove, and secondly, we can submit them to police station as our suspect for Grandmother's murder and ask them to investigate," said Rika as she sat on the couch reading a fashion magazine.

Arta was unable to hold back and added, "I don't know why; I felt they were telling the truth. Farhad appeared to be well-mannered, courteous, and somehow attractive."

Mother asked her to avoid meddling in matters that had nothing to do with her since she didn't like what she had to say.

I could see Arta's point that there was something special about him—not an enemy—in his gaze. My family should be grateful for what Mr. Clark's family has done for us over the years by waiting and letting us keep the house to ourselves, but sadly, as often, they didn't want to see the bright side of the story.

Chapter 13
Magenta

I was having nightmares about my grandmother and how she was killed. I was blaming myself for leaving her that day; I ought to have stayed with her.

I couldn't wait for the school results, which were due very soon. Every day, I spoke with Catherine over the phone about our ambitions and our hopes that Edwin would never return or that his journey would take longer than anticipated.

Unfortunately, because Mother and Rose were preoccupied with the court case, they followed Rika's advice! The court has given Mr. Farhad permission to own the home.

Aunt Rose had it easier because she already owned a home, but for us it was a tragedy because Dad was not in a position to offer a house, at least not right away. Neither sister knew what to do.

For me and herself, my mother spent all of our savings on clothes, shoes, and accessories so that we would look well in front of Ms. Elsa and Edwin. We were totally destroyed, and I felt awful for Dad.

We couldn't move immediately away, so Dad asked Mom to phone the lawyer and begged for some time instead of speaking.

Due to the accusation, the lawyer was unhappy with them and responded, "My client is quite cross, you're lucky I could convince him not to use your complaint over you, as he is currently living in the city. I'll make an effort to communicate with him and let you know his decision."

Mother was no longer herself; each day, she awaited the call from the attorney requesting that everyone leave the house immediately.

Me and Arta were on the silent side; we were unable to speak for fear that she might erupt at the slightest hint of conversation and keep hurling rubbish at us.

After all, I received the results and was granted admission to the university! The biggest and happiest news of my life, I was forbidden by my father from telling anyone about it. He advised me that it would be best if I could keep the situation a secret from the family for a while. For the first time, I got the impression that he genuinely wanted to help me.

As I mentioned before, he wanted to find another way to argue with my mother since he didn't want her to destroy my future any longer. Whatever it was, I didn't care! Arta assumed that I was crying due of our current circumstance, and my mother assumed that I was missing Edwin.

I danced that night while holding my books in my arm and signing to them. The best present ever. God, thank you.

Chapter 14
Tickle Me Pink

I had already begun making arrangements to get to the city. Normally, Catherine and I would get down and make a list of the items I should pack and then search through my closet to select appropriate attire.

Additionally, I was able to visit Ms. Jane while attending school several days in secret.

She was excited for me, very supportive, and helped me choose my courses. With my father's approval, she also picked a close-by hostel for me. The fact that none of these required money made my father happier, and he frequently said, "Wait until your mother discovers about all of these; she will definitely have a heart attack!"

When the bell rung one day while I was home alone, I went to open the gate to see Mr. Farhad. When he asked whether anyone was home, as if he couldn't see me, I responded, "My parents are out, Mom will be back soon, if you want to meet her, you may come in and wait."

He came upstairs and sat in the hallway, appearing pleased with my offer. To make him some tea, I went to the kitchen.

He had on a pair of blue jeans and a white T-shirt, and I also observed that his eyes were green. Even though I used to be one of the tallest students in my class, I believed he was much taller!

After drinking his tea, he said, "What's your age? Are you studying?"

Although I was unable to provide any information regarding the university, I did respond, "I'll be seventeen this year and I just finished from high school."

"Do you have any plans to continue your studies?" he inquired, grinning at me.

I smiled at him, but before I could respond, my mother entered and stopped me from telling a lie.

She was startled to see him, greeted him without even looking at him, and walked to the kitchen where I was standing to reprimand me for letting him in the house and what if he had killed me the same way he had killed Grandmother! Regarding her final sentence, I could not help but laugh!

"What motivated you to come and visit us?" she questioned as she sat down in front of him.

"Right now, I'm occupied with other things in my life, and I had delayed the project for this house for the following year, in order to give you enough time to hunt for a new place," Farhad answered.

When I swiftly signaled my silence to my mother when she tried to criticize him, she remarked, "Maybe by next year likewise, you will entirely give up on your idea and allow us to stay here and pay you the rent!"

I cannot imagine how difficult it was for her to simply say, "Thank you!"

As I walked Mr. Farhad out of the house, he advised me to consider pursuing further education and building a brighter future for myself. I don't understand why he was concerned about what my future would hold, but I valued his counsel.

I then questioned, "You won't come see us more often?"

He gently replied, "Let's see what the future has in store," and left.

When I walked into the house, Mother was furious as usual and yelled, "Why did you accompany him? You ought to have hugged him too and thanked him for deporting us from our home!"

"Who knows what will happen next year and why we should quarrel with him when he is trying to be nice to us?" I told her to calm down and at least he provided us the time that we all wanted.

She remained silent, so perhaps my remarks could help her to loosen a little.

Chapter 15
Shadow

The event I was worried about transpired; Edwin returned in the final week of my summer vacation and demanded to see me right away. Mother was ecstatic that he was still enquiring about me and had not developed feelings for someone else.

I was extremely disappointed, and my mother was my main challenge. I sincerely hoped Grandmother was still alive and could help me, but I lacked the strength to tell him to stop bothering me.

When my mother entered the room, I was hiding beneath a blanket and acting ill. She commanded me to stop, and to get ready for my future husband.

She was referring to him as my spouse even though we weren't even engaged. I wished someone had awakened her up and shown her the truth.

When I was about to leave the house, my mother again stopped me and asked, "Are you going to a funeral?" I had not dressed nicely; I was just in my casual clothes, a shirt and pants, and no makeup.

I told her I wouldn't go if she insisted, and when she got worried and said, "You're just as silly as your father." I wished she could realize why I was doing all of this. "If we are fortunate enough, he will marry you, purchase a home for each of us, provide free education for your brother, secure employment for your father, and much more. Don't forget that we don't have much time, so attempt to pressure him into getting married to you right away. Our final hope is in you."

My grandmother used to always say, "Reena is always in a rush to have everything over a night; she wants the easiest and fastest way of success and that made her life much harder." I wished she would let me help them in a different way because I was confident, I could help my family. However, she didn't want that.

Edwin was standing by the door when I left the house with a sizable arrangement of flowers. He now had a bizarre haircut that made him look slimmer, his face had completely transformed, and the area beneath his eyes was dark.

I simply thanked him when he kissed me and handed me flowers before he started talking in the car about his travels, parties, and new acquaintances.

He seemed very content.

We visited their old home as usual. Even though I told him no, he insisted that I stay the night. "We aren't even engaged, so please consider what people could say if they learned about us, I pleaded with him."

He began laughing so loudly as a result of what I said, which was quite unpleasant. Later, he came to his senses and declared, "Our family knows, and that is enough. There is no rush to be married because there is still much to do." He came, sat down on the sofa next to me, and unzipped the bag. There were many brand-name items, including two sets of diamond jewelry, which truly drew my eye but didn't impress me, along with clothing, shoes, and handbags in quantity.

I was simply too terrified to break up with him and admit that I was no longer in love with him. After that, I was unsure if he would have abandoned me alive.

He also observed my changes and kept asking me why I was acting so differently. I just said, "All these days, you were missing, suddenly, you came out of nowhere and begging me to be myself." Having regular conversation with him became very difficult for me. All that night, I was just silent.

"Why did you leave and where have you been lately?" I asked.

He just said, "I was forced to." His next move was to brew coffee in the kitchen. I avoided starting any fresh conversations with him by keeping quiet about the house and all that occurred while he was away.

"Have you met any other guys?" he inquired after bringing the coffee for me.

When I laughed this time, he became really irritated and spilled the entire cup of hot coffee on my feet. I jumped up and shouted, but he was simply gazing at me.

"Just a friendly reminder not to joke about with me and to be mindful of who you are speaking to!" he screamed.

I went straight to the bathroom, got the toothpaste, and applied some to the burned spot.

I cried to myself out of fear as I wondered what I could possibly do to him. I was a tool in a relationship that was largely between my mother and Edwin, and there was no way out. I knew that if I started disputing with him, he would hurt me even more.

As a result, when I exited the restroom, I saw him waiting for me while sitting on the sofa and holding the diamond sets in his hands.

"You don't understand what I went through while you were away." So I giggled while acting as if nothing had happened.

"My love, did I traumatize you, believe me, the only guy in the world I want to be with is you, day and night I waited for you to come back. I was terrified if you had found someone else and completely neglected me."

After hearing what I had to say, he approached me, grabbed my hand, drew me to him, and placed the diamond sets in my hand, saying, "Even the queen of France doesn't have this."

He dropped me up at my house an hour later. My mother was overjoyed to see all the gifts, especially the diamonds, which caused her to shout and ask, "Ariana, do you realize how much each of them costs? Oh my God, I can't believe it." She immediately hurried to get Arta to come down and see everything.

She was completely unaware of my limp. I went to my room and began berating myself for my weakness in enabling him to treat me this way and for not being more resilient. I was simply asking God to make it so I could get rid of him. I was feeling bad since, according to my mother, I was their only chance, so what would happen to my family if I left him?

Chapter 16
Desert Sand

Every day, Edwin would pick me up in the morning and leave me off in the evening. We frequented many gatherings, including restaurants and concerts. He made me meet his mother one day because he said I had to get her blessing if I wanted to get married to him.

That day, Edwin demanded a lot, and his mother, acting as though she wanted to buy something, said that she should check her calendar and let us know if there was any chance, we might get engaged, but marriage was out of the question.

The head of our school, Ms. Jane, introduced me to the group that was fighting any injustice toward women. It was amusing that Ms. Elsa, Edwin's mother, was also its founder!

Ms. Jane informed me that this was being done to ensure that even if my father changes his mind after signing all the documents, this group will be able to assist me in retaining my rights as a member of their community and making decisions regarding my own future.

I wasn't sure if joining this organization was the right decision, but I was prepared to stand up for myself, especially after Edwin returned and became bossier. Even in front of his mother, he was about to slap me, and she was just acting as though she didn't see anything or didn't want to get concerned!

My offer letter had already come, and the hostel approval was also there. Everything was ready, except for me. Dad was not yet permitting me to reveal the university matter.

I was sick of acting, sick of all the gatherings, guests, dresses, cosmetics. I just wanted peace, I just wanted to be myself again, and I didn't want a partner in my life, but the words my mother kept saying in my ear every time I met Edwin, gave me anxiety!

There were no signs of packing or even the beginning of a search for a new home. Everyone, even Benjamin, was waiting for me to be married before looking for a higher career or even a house for his. It was ludicrous!

I could have simply refused the entire Edwin situation, but I was afraid of my mother's response and the massive argument she would start with my father! How did it happen that I was suddenly given such importance in the family?

Even Arta had changed totally; she could see I wasn't happy, but she never tried to find out why. Catherine was the only one I could trust to talk to, so at least that made me happy.

A large party was about to take place. The town was discussing Edwin's parents' anniversary at the time. Although my family was anticipating the announcement of our wedding, Edwin told me he desired to make our engagement official that day.

Dad finally made up his mind and declared, "As a father of Ariana, I don't accept and bless any engagement," after daily arguments between Mom and Dad in the home.

Mom said, "No one is seeking for your permission since, Ariana has made up her mind already and she intends to marry the love of her life and I don't let anybody to step in front of them," as if she didn't care what Dad was feeling at all.

Chapter 17
Inch Worm

"Oh my God, you are more dazzling than ever tonight!" Edwin's mother.

I was already worn out after our first dance and didn't want anyone to call or bother me any longer. Mother was speaking with Ms. Elsa, Arta and Rose were disputing with Mr. Harold in the hallway about the curtain colors, and as usual, Rose was with Mr. Jack.

I wished the entire night that Edwin would be occupied and stop asking for me.

When Edwin's cousin Zack approached, I could tell because every time I spoke to him or let him sit at our table, Edwin and I would get into a heated argument, with the outcome being a gift of one smack for me.

I'm not sure why I believed that my boyfriend or future husband had every right to raise his hand at me because I had witnessed it happening so frequently in our town and it became a normal part of marital life.

He asked if he could chat to me while I pretended to be looking for something in my handbag. I said, "I'm sorry, but Edwin doesn't allow me to welcome you to our table, my apologies."

While Edwin was making his way to the stage to unveil our engagement, he drew closer to me, pretending to need a drink of water before bending over and warning me to run away because Edwin had a serious illness and is potentially dangerous. "Last month, they traveled to Paris for his medication, and he was admitted to a mental hospital."

My heart was beating faster, and I could feel my chicks burning, when all of a sudden, I heard everyone was congratulating me!

We don't have much time left for any more games and playdates, so why has he announced engagement rather than a wedding, wondered my mother.

I felt like I was about to pass out and I wanted to shout for help and end this relationship. I was shaking when Arta arrived and hugged me; I told her we should leave; she became irritated and shouted, "Stop being so foolish and behave normal! This is the outcome that we were all hoping for."

The only thing I could hear in my brain that night was Zack's voice telling me to 'protect yourself'. That night, I cried a lot, and everybody assumed that I was sobbing tears of happiness.

On the drive home, my mother was berating me nonstop, yelling in the vehicle, "Why couldn't you hide your dreadful feeling in front of everyone? You were sobbing like though you were waiting for Edwin to propose to you."

Rika laughed and gave me an idiotic look. "Evidently, a girl in her position couldn't even imagine Edwin dancing with her, let alone proposing to her."

I hoped I could have opened up and told them everything, but my family didn't encourage me to do so. How could I convey my emotions? I was so devastated that I believed my life was over.

I felt as though all of my university aspirations had vanished.

The following day, my parents fought a lot as usual, but this time, Dad had already taken the necessary steps and announced that I had been accepted to the university, so I would be going in less than a month.

I quickly offered my mother a drink of water, but she dropped it, smacked me, and started talking crazy! Mom became so agitated, she shouted so loudly, and she began smashing all the plates and cups that were on the table. It was a very frightening situation.

Mother informed Arta everything when she came downstairs due to the commotion! She was astonished as well, and at first, she was angry with me for keeping it from her. However, I saw her smiling at me while my mother was distracted.

Thankfully, my father maintained his composure and merely watched the drama at that time. He had planned to get revenge on his wife since he was so enraged inside, and this may have been the only or best method to do so.

She didn't settle down until the next day, and when Dad departed an hour later, I was the only one still at home and got the lecture.

Mom warned me that if Edwin finds out, he will undoubtedly leave me and call off the engagement. I must resign right away. This time, I spoke up for myself and said, "Fine, this is precisely how I want; he is dealing with some personal problems, he is ill, and he is not who you assume he is!"

Arta stopped my mother from throwing the vase at me, and she screamed, "Shame on you! All those times when you were going out with him, dressed up, and having fun, he was not having any problems. Have you forgotten that he was your dream and that you were longing to be with him? We reside in a tiny town; what would people say if you two weren't wed? I can't continue to live here; if I do, your family and I will be ashamed, just like Rose and Rika were."

Arta sent her to her room to rest after she started crying again. When she returned, she sat next to me and said, "I don't know what to say; I am glad for you, sad, and terrified at the same time; Mother is right, and you are right as well. I don't know to take who's side!"

I explained to her everything that had happened, including why I hadn't told them earlier and how my father had come up with the plan to continue working. She was merely listing, but I know she was picturing her family future in between.

"Arta, please help me. Edwin is abusing me, and I don't want to be with him." She urged me to elaborate when she became alarmed.

"He is ill, I can't even speak to him, and his aggressiveness, rudeness, incivility, and truculence are no longer under control."

Then I told her what he had done to me over those months.

She called these severe problems and chastised me for not telling her sooner. "The only thing left to do if your relationship has reached this point is to enroll in college. This will give you some breathing room while we decide what to do. However, I can't guarantee that I can help with Mother," she added.

Although she was unsure of what would happen, she offered for me to come upstairs and remain with them until Mother was settled.

Chapter 18
Beaver

The following day, I called Ms. Jane and informed her about the engagement and my mother's reaction to my enrollment at the university. She urged me to cool off and strictly adhere to her directions and promised to speak with my father shortly.

She reassured me that I should not be concerned since I am protected because I am registered with their group (the one that looks out for women's rights).

Edwin kept calling my mother to want to see me. I made the decision to meet him and tell him everything on my own. He wanted to take me on a short trip to the countryside, but I objected and said, "We just got engaged. Traveling together at this point is not appropriate." Also, I informed him that Dad was not happy with me getting married so soon. "He wants me to go to the university."

He didn't like what I said, as usual, and hit me in the chest. I fell to the ground after being knocked back into the wall, and nobody was around to watch us that day.

Once again slapping me, he added, "Tell your foolish father it is too late to be dogmatic about his daughter. From now on, I own you and he can't do anything about it. Your mother has sold you to me and we have an agreement so either I get you or her." I instantly stood up.

That day, as I went alone home, I wondered how I might pull myself out of this predicament. It was so terrifying that I was willing to do anything to end this agonizing life. On the night of my birthday, when I had just turned seventeen, he hit me.

Zack was right; when he was beating me, his eyes were unable to perceive anything else, making him dangerous and ill as well. Arta warned him that if he hit me again, I would have to strike back, so he knew I wouldn't continue to stand by and do nothing.

I guess I wasn't a very good fighter, he was out of control, and I finally snapped. When I got home, no one remembered it was my birthday and Catherine was the only one who wished me that night. I was relieved to receive Catherine's call right when I needed to. We both cried that night, and she assured me she would pray for me to rapidly get over this horrible time.

Prior to our lunchtime appointment, I chose to meet Ms. Jane. I was supposed to see Edwin.

She welcomed me with a great hug and said, "Your father was here the other day. We talked a lot, or perhaps we argued a lot. I told him you had a team to defend you going forward. He was glad, but not for you, mostly to hurt your mother's spirit. In the end, we made the decision to discuss your case during our gathering with the community this evening. Ms. Elsa will be there and I'm sure she'll be surprised to hear your name, so I needed to get your consent before I did anything else."

I informed her that Edwin is a dangerous person and that my mother is not at all encouraging, asking me to resign already.

She warned me that the situation would be a little tricky because my mother and my fiancé would need to be informed, but she urged me to be hopeful.

I gave her permission to speak on my behalf, and if it was necessary, I could join them as well. However, I begged her to watch over me.

After our catch-up, I went to see Edwin. He was occupied these days, so when we would run into one other at restaurants. I was unable to eat anything at the restaurant since my thoughts were diverted by the evening meeting.

I reasoned that I should inform him about us and the institution before he hears from his mother, but when I saw those terrified eyes, I had to keep my mouth sealed.

I wasn't expecting Edwin to drop me off so soon because he had to leave with his father for some business meetings.

I went to the roof, sat down, and briefly closed my eyes, wishing I had never entered that party or any other locations that my mother had asked me to see! She wasn't the only one at fault; I was also at failure since I desired him too much to consider the facts. There was no escape for me from my blind loving prison!

Chapter 19
Midnight Blue

I had slept off on the roof when Arta called my name. It was dark and chilly, and she questioned, "Do you know what time it is?"

"Is that important?" I asked as I turned to face her.

"Edwin brought you a cake and a ton of birthday presents, but we were unable to locate you, so he left. Of course, it's vital!" She responded, "We were all concerned about what had happened to you; he thought you were at Catherine's." She then urged me to go phone him because he will be concerned.

I was staying at Arta's place when she called his number and handed me the phone. After telling him where I was, he still didn't believe me and ended the call.

The meeting was successful, tomorrow everyone will know, even the press will write about it, congratulations, Dad remarked as he came to hug me at Arta's house where he was also there when my mother was hosting a VIP guest (Edwin).

When Arta asked father what he was talking to me about, he tried to divert the issue and replied, "I am a proud parent, Ariana will be the first girl to attend to the university from our town."

"I thought she was going to resign, but Mom said she has already notified her," exclaimed Arta. Infuriated, Dad warned her not to bring up Mother or her foolish views ever again and reprimanded Arta for failing to be encouraging.

Analia, Arta's kid, was playing with some soft toys that I was certain Edwin had brought for her, so I knelt down next to her and attempted to occupy myself with her.

I spent the night in Analia's room. In the middle of the night, Arta woke me up. As she yanked me out of bed, she exclaimed, "There are police officers downstairs waiting to talk to me!" I was scared.

We both went together; I noticed that Dad was waiting outside and that Mom was reporting on her activities for the previous twenty-four hours.

When the officer approached, she questioned, "Ariana, am I right?" She added, "Regrettably, your friend Catherine was murdered in front of her gate a few hours ago. After speaking with her parents, they indicated that you were the only person who knew her, as well as the last person she had spoken to."

I can't even begin to describe how I felt when I found that my best and only friend had been killed. I sat on the ground, clamped my mouth shut as I yelled her name and felt lost without her. She was so innocent; who could do anything like that!

The police muttered something to my father before they all departed, and Arta, who was also crying, urged them to leave me alone so I could gather myself.

Mother went away while muttering, "That girl seemed strange to me from the first, she was up to no good, and see what happened to her."

"Her dad is my buddy, can you please stop what you have been doing these days," Dad shouted at her. "Catherine is dead, the girl who has been with Ariana since preschool! I scarcely know you anymore, so shame on you for speaking that negatively about her."

I'm unable to talk about the evening because I had a such a horrible, unexpected birthday surprise! I simply knew Arta was giving me various medications and trying to put me to sleep.

The cops came again the following day, but this time they were only interested in leaving after I had provided their inquiries.

I informed them of what I knew about her, including the fact that she had never had a boyfriend and that although her family wanted her to be married after high school, she was unable to select a suitable partner. She lived such a straightforward life—no ups and downs—that there wasn't much else I could tell them.

Grandmother's murder was also brought up by the police, who noted that 'less than a year has passed and there has already been a second murder'.

"Good for you, folks, it can keep you occupied for a while and give the murderer time to arrange the next one," my mother exclaimed.

She was correct—unfortunately, the lawsuit involving my grandma was still pending, as was the second!

We were all wondering who could have done such a thing as the investigating team left our home.

I received a call from Ms. Elsa asking me to join their team in the evening at the town hall and asking my parents, particularly my dad, to join. Edwin had not communicated as he had previously stated that he needed to attend to a few business matters with his father.

Mother was surprised and inquired as to whether I had lately argued with Edwin again. Since I didn't want to explain myself to her and risk receiving another reprimand at the time—I was still reeling from the loss of my friend—I simply said, "If you'd like, you can come with me and find out yourself," and I went to my room.

What has happened to my dear Catherine? We were meant to remain together until the end; why did you leave me and break your commitments? How can I breathe without you? I'll never quit moaning for you...

Chapter 20
Chestnut

My father demanded we attend the meeting despite the fact that I was unable to even stand upright. My mother was also getting ready to accompany us because she was quite interested in seeing what all the excitement was about. Dad spoke to her and I overheard him saying, "We are going to see who the community who's leader is Ms. Elsa, so please don't do or say anything dumb, which you will end up regretting." Then he glanced at me and blinked!

Men made all of the significant decisions in our community, which implies that they were the only ones who could work, attend college, join any sports team, or even be picked for key government positions! Being that we were living in the twenty-first century at the time made things incredibly odd. Unexpectedly, our town was uneasy and would have tolerated these laws continuously.

I wanted to be alone but was unable to since I was puzzled, not in the mood for any surprise, and confused.

No one was conversing in the car, but after we arrived at the school hall where the gathering was to take place, I noticed that Catherine's large photograph was surrounded by countless flowers and candles.

It was a really emotional time, and I couldn't contain my tears. As we entered the meeting room, Ms. Jane, the school's principal, entered wearing all-black clothing and no makeup.

At the table, there were six additional women, one of which was Ms. Elsa. We were instructed to sit after she declined Mom's request to go shake hands with her.

They all made introductions. Our sole contacts were Ms. Jane and Ms. Elsa.

Mom asked, "Can somebody clarify what is this all about and why are we here?" as she was clearly unsure of what was going on.

"You are here today to be proof of the inquiry, our community has arrived to the decision for the case of Ms. Ariana," one woman who appeared more mature said.

"What is your community accountable for, and why have you called us," she enquired. The same woman then gave her all the information she required.

My father forbade my mother from asking any further questions because she was still seeming startled.

"Ms. Ariana, we are happy to let you know that our community will protect all of your rights from the beginning to the finish of your experience at university," the woman stated. "Our team made all the preparations, and our coordinator, Ms. Elsa, agreed to cover any additional expenses that the university did not cover out of her own pocket."

Mom was showing signs of disbelief, while we were listening to them so quietly.

This time, Ms. Jane got up and congratulated me on the new chapter in life. "When you are older, you will reflect on this period of your life and realize that it marked a significant turning point in your career. Take in the pleasure of countless options for your existence. Explore. Think. Cherish the day and be yourself! Although getting into law school is difficult, you have shown that nothing is impossible. Well done, kid," she spoke.

Then everyone applauded for me, and Ms. Jane came over to give me a hug. Ms. Elsa wasn't happy, but she tried to smile, and my mother was triffid and on the verge of exploding.

Mother went to Ms. Jane and told her, "Ariana is my child; I am the one who will decide for her. You are an awful lady from the inside out; you have no power to make decisions for her."

She then turned around and said to Ms. Elsa, "You very well knew my daughter was about to marry your son in a limited timeframe, why did you consent to such dreadful plan, have you ignored all your commitments?"

All of the other members were looking at Ms. Elsa, which made it difficult for her to feel comfortable answering the query. "With all due respect, Ms. Reena, I would prefer not to discuss any family matters at this meeting. We are all professionals working to support your daughter, so please be grateful," Ms. Elsa replied to Mother.

My mother was ordered to leave the hallway by two security guards who were stationed at the door. At first, she protested, but my father led her out so that she wouldn't cause any trouble. I was feeling miserable for her.

The woman who spoke at the beginning of the meeting told me, "My dear, with a mother like that, you truly need our support. Please don't hesitate to phone any of us at any time of the day, and after ten days, a car will come and pick you up and leave you off at hustle."

Throughout my entire existence, I had been awaiting this time; it was my dream, and I had been getting ready for it, so why wasn't I joyful any longer? My feelings were non-existent, I couldn't hear, and it was pitch black. Was it due of Catherine's passing, or my supposedly adoring fiancé, who would undoubtedly kill me once I left this area, or even my obdurate mother? My grandmother's passing was an important part of the narrative that I overlooked.

Both good and unpleasant things happened to me at the same moment. I wished I could turn invisible and temporarily hide from everyone. I required some alone time in order to observe my surroundings. I wasn't feeling well.

Mom and Dad were arguing as usual, but this time it was louder and more intense! I was the lone witness to their previous conflicts, so Arta asked me, what have I done again?

Adam stopped communicating to me during those times because his peers teased him for being my brother, I was known as the town's 'lost skirt', and he was embarrassed to even be in the same room as me. As a result, we hardly ever saw each other.

Both Adam and Arta began berating me once they heard the tale from our mother. I was so puzzled at the time that I was unable to respond to what they were saying and was even unable to hear them.

As always, Dad was overjoyed and pleased that his plans had come to fruition. I just automatically followed him to the terrace as he lit up his cigar and I asked, "Dad, is this what you hoped? Since this is exactly the reverse of what I had in mind. How should I proceed?" I quizzed him.

He remarked, "My relationship with your mother has come to an end. She shattered my identity when she sacrificed my daughter to another woman's son in exchange for wealth and power," as he sat on the chair with his spectacles on top of his head.

"She never saw how hard I was working to keep this family happy. I had a vision for each of my children. She cannot be the lady I married or the one I once loved. I really tried to get her to listen to me, but she has turned into her daughter's adversary and instead went and sold my house's contents to a friend of mine, to purchase party attire and jewelry. Your mom made me feel guilty.

"Your grandmother summoned me downstairs on the day she was murdered and requested me to keep this a secret. She urged me to assist you in getting to university and I vowed to do so under all circumstances. She stated Reena already has wrecked Arta's future and Adam's mentality, but I still have one child to save, and that child is you.

"I did everything I could to help you; now you must make your own decisions."

Oh my God, I misjudged my own father all these days because he was a man of his words. I thought he was enjoying the battles.

Chapter 21
Razzle Dazzle Rose

Things didn't get back to normal for a few days; Dad did everything in his power to avoid Mom and only return home for bedtime.

Mother kept calling Ms. Elsa to ask her to reject the idea of me attending university. I realized the last time she called her, Ms. Elsa cut the conversation, and after that, she never returned any of her calls. She was ignoring her every time.

Benjamin had already begun seeking for employment when one of their family friends assisted him in finding one. Although the position was in the south of the country with a tropical climate, he had accepted it. Arta was constantly complaining and accusing me for everything. Surprising, Edwin stopped calling and bothering me, I had a week to be prepared.

I once went grocery shopping with Arta, and as we were returning, Edwin asked if he might spend some time with me. I begged Arta to say no, but she consented. He then dropped Arta off at home and, as usual, drove me to the old house.

He repeatedly beat me when I refused to enter, and after abusing me as usual while I was inside, he left. Let's not discuss how I was feeling at the time.

After an hour, he returned, as joyful as ever, and instructed me to get ready before joining him.

I was given a glass of drink after purring, "Have you seen all your revealing images, you look gorgeous in them. I can't wait until I show them to your father." He laughed loudly.

When I started sobbing and pleading with him not to do that, he grabbed my hair and growled, "Now you're asking people to come save you from me! Who has permitted you to enroll in college, I won't allow you to put a step forward." He kicked me so forcefully that I fell on the ground.

I got to my feet and shouted, "You are one sick, immoral evil. Zack had warned me about your mental illness. I know who you are. I know why you fled and went to Paris."

Then I escaped and found refuge in the restroom. He pursued me and attempted to force open the door; however, the doors had two lucks and were made of metal, making it difficult for him to gain entry.

My body was shaking, and I was so terrified that I wanted to throw up. I searched for something sharp to use as protection in case he tried to attack me, but I was unsuccessful.

After some time, he gave up and said, "If you want to go to the university, you have to do something for me. In exchange, I'll swear not to disturb you ever again and I'll also trash all the pictures. Call Zack and invite him over for a drink at the old house, please. All I ask from you is this, and you will then be set free forever."

Why did he want Zack and I to go there? What did he intend? Oh my Lord, please assist me—how am I going to escape this situation?

How or why should I put my trust in him? If I had to risk someone else's life in order to preserve mine, I would sooner die than cause anyone any harm.

The bathroom window was open, but I was on the second floor and unsure of what was on the other side, though I knew I could pass through it. I was attempting to find a way out of that area.

I first pretended to be crying in a loud voice so he wouldn't think twice about me running away. Then, despite the fact that my nose was bleeding, I used the trash can to climb the wall. Climbing a marble wall was really challenging.

The fact that the house was on an old plot of land may have been its only saving grace at the time. Although leaping from a great height was not something I was skilled at, I nevertheless did it without considering where I would land. My arm and leg were definitely fractured, and it took me some time to put my pieces back together because it was so dark that I could hardly see anything.

The gate was locked; however, the walls weren't very tall. I was suffering, but I didn't want to hesitate, so I climbed a tree, leaped on a wall from there, and finally landed on the ground.

I can't even remember how long I ran before I reached the main road. I threw myself in front of the first car as it approached from a distance and motioned for it to stop. I asked the couple to aid me and then fell once the car stopped and they both got out.

Chapter 22
Tumbleweed

I'm not sure how long I was asleep, but when I opened my eyes, my father's face was the first one I noticed. He was holding my hand and looking at me when I overheard him calling out to the nurse to let her know I was awake.

Two nurses came together and had shocked looks on their faces. They took the tubes out of my throat with difficulties, making it appear as though they weren't anticipating me to awaken too early. I had discomfort in my left arm and leg, making it hard for me to move. I was still oblivious to my situation. I was simply thinking about how long I had been sleeping at the time.

"Hello, my love, we are extremely relieved to see you awake. It is a marvel that you are still alive. Regretfully, your left arm has a fracture, but your leg merely has a break that is primarily on the ankle side," a nurse said.

"Unfortunately, there was internal bleeding that we could stop early, and two of your ribs were damaged as well," she added as she lifted my leg higher than my body. "You have been asleep for forty-eight hours, and a couple brought you to the hospital. Fortunately, one of the security guards recognized you, which allowed us to locate your parents since he used to be Ms. Elsa's driver. I guess it's not always horrible to live in a tiny town!"

I don't know if I was crying out of joy or because I was hurt. She gave me an explanation of the hospital's procedure for dealing with a case like mine before requesting that I provide the police with some information in accordance with hospital policy.

Father came and hugged me, and said, "I can't even imagine you have opened your eyes, they only let one person stay with you. I've known for a long time that animal won't just watch you go to college. I found out through Arta that she had authorized him to take you away. Despite the fact that I had told the police everything, they initially had doubts.

"They have finally begun hunting for him since yesterday after making such persistent requests. It appears like the entire family has packed up and flown to Paris for the evening! Police are everywhere looking for him." My father appeared terrible because he was so irate and worn out.

"How much longer till I depart for university?" I murmured.

"Five days more, my child." He patted my head.

I gave him a grin while averting my gaze.

I could be discharged tomorrow, but I need to give a full explanation of the entire tragedy that has occurred to me, the nurse told me.

I truly wanted to avoid talking about the entire situation, but I was compelled to.

I recognized the police officer since she handled the matter involving my grandma and Catherine's. She approached me and gave me a pitying look before saying, "Hi, Ariana, I'm sorry about what happened to you. I need you to help me this time, because this guy—whoever he is—tried to end your life, and now that he knows you are living, he will return for you to complete what he had begun. Ariana, if you could speak with us, I need to know everything, because what occurred to you was unfair."

Since there were only the two of us in the room, she went to lock the door, returned, sat on the chair, and said, "Ariana, he has been physically abusing you; you have been hurt," in a louder voice. "The doctor said you had previously fractured ribs, so why did you let him do all of this to you and why didn't you ask for help? Kindly assist yourself. Were you coerced to remain with him, and did any of your family members help him?"

I had no control over the shaking in my body, so she held me in her arm till I was calm. I informed her, looking into her eyes, "I was pushed down this path at first; I was only sixteen when I met him. He has medical records from the Paris psychological hospital and is dangerous as well as very ill."

One of the police officers interrupted us and requested her to go outside so she could answer a critical phone call.

After returning, she apologized and said, "I have to leave right away, but I'll be back shortly. Apparently, Mr. Zack, the conductor of the symphony, has gone missing."

I tried to stop her, but she left the room and I was unable to shout because my throat was still hurting. I only managed to drop the water glass that was on my table before I saw her racing back inside and asking, "Are you okay, my dear?"

I filled her in on everything that happened that day, including Edwin's scheme to get Zack to the old house. She instructed me to tell them the address, but as I only knew the major route, she chose to accompany me instead.

When they eventually located the house, my father and I were both in the ambulance, and I was holding my father's hand tightly because I was terrified that Edwin would open the door and leap inside.

The investigating team had their dogs with them, so they were able to locate Zack's grave immediately.

Fortunately, he was still alive, though severely injured. His wrists and legs were also firmly fastened to a large piece of wood, which was scary. "I am proud of you, Ariana, you saved his life. I know you are in a terrible agony, but you made sure to come and help." My father kissed my forehead and murmured.

I just passed out in the ambulance due to being so fatigued.

Chapter 23
Unmellow Yellow

I had returned home, but nothing was as it had been. Arta was not allowed to visit me, Mother was constantly crying, and Adam avoided me as usual as he's never felt anything for me.

Due to my health, I was staying at my grandmother's house, and being there brought back all of my memories of her.

In some way, father was blaming Aunt Rose and Rika for breaking our family, so Mother asked them not to bother me for a while.

Three different nurses were switching shifts throughout the day and night as they came to our house daily from the hospital.

I heard that my father sold his vehicle to finance the cost of the hospital stay and the comprehensive treatment program. I was shocked by the amount of suffering I had brought this family. I preferred quietness and only spoke to people if I had a need. I didn't want to bring up a topic only to get into an argument over it.

Since I was the one doing everything in the house all the time and wanted to still be in room while eating three meals, including snacks, Mother tried to prepare various things for me to eat in bed. To be honest, I had never been treated as well as this.

When I cried for Catherine and prayed for my grandmother, I wished I had someone to talk to. The hospital gave me an electric wheelchair so I wouldn't have to use both of my hands, and the nurses helped me learn how to use it for a day.

Father advised me to skip the first term because it might take some time for me to heal. I decided I didn't want to wait any longer and was physically prepared to get to my favorite place.

Mom kept apologizing and asked me to tell her everything that happened that day so she could hasten my recovery, which I doubted.

There was no longer any trust between us, and I knew she would have used the tale to punish me in some way.

Likewise, I was only grinning at her while attempting to remain silent. Even though the experience was neither new nor strange to me, it was obviously difficult for them to accept the truth, so I refrained from sharing anything with them. Remembering the times when I begged her to assist me in getting rid of him but, tragically, she never once heard me.

As before, I had packed my bags, and Catherine had assisted me in gathering my cabin essentials.

A night before I depart, Arta came down to be with me. She did her best to act normally and not to remind me of anything. We chatted about how much fun we used to have as kids. She also stated that she will visit.

"Don't expect me to come down tomorrow; it's sad to see you go, but there's something I need to tell you: I'm so happy for my sister that she's starting college, and I'm also jealous of and dissatisfied in myself. You were very lucky because at least you knew there are some individuals to keep you safe. In my time, I didn't fight enough and I wasn't even aware of my rights. Simply walking in my mother's footsteps, I did."

I held her hand and comforted her, saying, "You can still complete your education if you wish. There are lots of individuals in universities and colleges who are married and have children as well. You should ask Benjamin to assist you, perhaps."

She hugged me, which hurt my fractured ribs, and then she thanked me and added, "I wish I had your talent. You always find better side of almost everything, which has made you exceptional and wonderful."

I finally got the day I had been waiting for, but unhappily I was unable to use the car that had been prearranged, so a van took me to my hostel instead.

On the other side, my mother was so agitated and combative that I felt she had lost a lot of weight recently and also appeared older than her age. Dad was accompanying me because I truly needed his support.

I encouraged her to quit blaming herself because there was nothing we could do about the past and to instead focus on building a better future. There was a nurse in the van with us when I started crying and telling my mother, "I love you, Mom, and I'm so sorry I failed you and smashed your dreams, since those were something which were not created for me." She begged me to calm down because any form of stress may easily affect my breathing.

Once I'm feeling better, I'll continue to see her, I kissed her hand and promised.

Seven hours of driving made me nervous and unsure of what to anticipate. Around four in the afternoon, we arrived there. The nurse waited in the car with me while my father went to double-check everything and grab the key. My room was on the second level, but Ms. Jane just obtained a request to move it.

Father began removing the baggage, and the nurse was assisting me in descending. I begged her to let me go up to the room by myself because I couldn't use crutches because of my broken ribs on one side and my arm and leg in a cast on the other. Sincerity be damned, the anguish was beyond what I could stand, yet I was fighting.

Since everything had already been planned, there weren't many students about at that time, and I could simply travel to my cabin. There was only enough space in the room for a bed and a cupboard.

As she approached the front gate, Ms. Marble, the lady in charge of the dormitory, exclaimed, "Welcome, my dear, I am so sorry to see you in this situation, but at the same time I'm pleased to have you here. You've shown that nothing can stop you from achieving your goals."

She continued, "The janitor's room was the only room on the ground floor with a private bathroom; she was so kind, she permitted you to use her room until you will be able to go to your own room."

It was time to say goodbye to my dad. We were both trying to hold back our emotions and control our tears, but there was a big smile at the end when he assured me everything is gonna be alright, and then he left after giving me a great cuddle.

"Anything urgent, you can just shout," Ms. Marble remarked, "my room is up front." I thanked her for helping me out.

I am now officially a college student, sitting in my own desk. Oh my God!

After all that I had to endure to get here, I wasn't sure how I should feel. That evening, I made a pledge to myself that my currier would be the only thing I would concentrate on.

Chapter 24
Blush

I was the last person to leave the room because getting dressed on my own was challenging, but I made a huge effort to appear normal and refuse assistance from everyone.

Ms. Marble came to check on me to make sure everything was well, and when she saw that my classes were being held on the first floor without a wheelchair facility, she informed me that it would have been simpler if I could have walked with my crutches.

It was a relief that my father had left me crutches. Ms. Marble informed me that almost every preparation had been made for my comfort, so I was overjoyed to see a buggy prepared outside for me.

The driver of the buggies requested me to wait for him at the same location after my lessons when he left me off in front of the building.

I asked security for assistance in locating my classes, and Ms. Marble was correct—they were on the first floor.

Students were passing by and offering assistance, but I was turning them all down till I eventually made it to class after much struggle. I think everyone had noticed that I was breathing hard by the time I located my seat, which was in the corner right by the door.

The first subject was legal research and writing, and the boy sitting next to me introduced himself as Mohammed and made an effort to be amiable. He said, "I had a broken leg past year, I know it is not easy to deal with, let me know if you ever need anything to make you feel more comfortable." He informed me.

I gave him my name, thanked him for the offer, I didn't feel like speaking to any boy or even girl of my type at the time.

Except for a few girls who were attempting to flaunt their designer handbags and the newest makeup, the class was silent. There were more than twenty students in that class, all of them were new like me.

When the master entered, I initially believed I was mistaken; but, as he introduced himself, there was no question that it was Mr. Farhad who was arranging to have us removed from either our home or his home! The world is so little, my goodness.

After calling for the register, he noticed, but I don't think he initially realized it was me. He tried to act normally and didn't respond.

Mohammed asked me if I needed anything from the canteen during the break because it was on the bottom floor, and I had trouble getting there. Although I was actually starving, I told him that I was alright because I didn't want to start a friendship with a boy right away.

Farhad was busy tidying up his desk before leaving. He briefly looked up to see whether anyone else was in the room, then he screamed, "Wish you a speedy recovery, and I'll be in touch," before leaving.

I was happy to recognize a familiar face there. I was too hungry to refuse Mohammed's offer of a cupcake and a bottle of milk when he returned.

The class that day concluded quickly, and I returned to my chalet before dark. After a few seconds, Ms. Marble entered and said, "Since we are neighbors, I really don't like to eat alone, so I thought there might be dinner we can have together." I knew Ms. Marble was the only one who could store food containers there.

I told her, "It is my honor to share a supper with a nice lady like you, especially since I am missing my mother's cuisine," feeling relieved to see so many good hearts around me.

When the lunch was eaten, she intended to depart, but not before she stated, "There is a phone in my room, which was used by janitor, it is only one way, that implies, they can call you internally or if my family calls, from operators they can link it to you and that is once a week."

I thanked her for the delicious supper. Later, I decided to take a quick shower, and given how I was feeling, it nearly took me two hours to get ready!

After taking a shower, I struggled to get dressed and was in severe pain; unhappily, all painkillers made me drowsy, so I avoided using them throughout the day. However, I took two pills and fell asleep as soon as I kept my head on the pillow. Sleeping was the thing I could do the quickest at that time, so I believe I was too comfy there!

Chapter 25
Vivid Violet

I successfully completed one week, albeit it was a hardship for me due to my health. Nevertheless, I did my best to ignore it. Everyone must have grown accustomed to seeing things that way because they stopped asking questions.

On Saturday, my mother called to let me know that she would be visiting me with Arta. I reasoned that the backyard had a large party hall for a family, making it the ideal location to spend time with them.

They arrived the following day, we gathered in the party hall, enjoyed ourselves, and Arta requested Ms. Marble to stay for a lunch that my mother had prepared and brought from home.

We discussed my academics, the students, and their persistent inquiries about my conditions. Little Analia was there as well, which really kept me busy; it was so soothing to carry her in my arm.

Since the staff housing, which Benjamin is offered, is already equipped, Arta said they would be moving in the next week and that she had only packed their clothes. She was unsure of how things would play out, but she seemed to have accepted the new circumstances. I concurred that she got off to a wonderful start.

Mother had undergone a lot of changes; she barely spoke to me but still inquired as to my needs and comfort in my room. I remarked, "Thanks to Ms. Marble, I have a wonderful dinner every night, and my room has a bathroom and a tiny shower, which is making it very convenient."

Mom and Arta thanked her for her assistance before she left us on our own. "I want to let you ladies know that me and your father have chosen to get a divorce. We thought this will be best for both of us." Mother wanted to talk to us but didn't know how to start.

I don't know why, but when we heard that, we were not at all startled. Arta was more worried about how she would break the news to Benjamin and his parents. "What about Adam? Who will he be with?" I questioned.

She retorted, "Your father will take care of him, but he needs extra attention because he's a heroin addict!"

It was quite distressing to learn that our only brother was doing drugs at such a young age. For a while, there was silence. I suppose we were all imagining the future.

"So where is Dad going to reside and what about you?" Arta questioned this time.

Mom responded, "Your father is going to rent an apartment close to his bakery, and Adam will spend a few months in a rehabilitation facility. Until I get a job and can rent a room for myself, I shall stay with Rose."

I couldn't believe the woman, who was wearing one of her expensive dresses to a party a few months ago, flashing her jewelry and the newest fashion, was now searching for a place to stay and a day job to pay for her meals. She was depressed and absolutely helpless, and I was unable to assist.

She sobbed and blamed herself for the breakdown of the family, claiming that she was unable to maintain our unity because she was a woman. I promised her that I would talk to father and ask him to think over the situation again.

She grabbed my hand and confessed, "I've damaged him, broken his spirit as a man. I believed I could make this family proud by you marrying that animal, but I was blind and ended up losing everything and everyone instead. These are things no one can fix."

I don't know what happened to me, but after hearing the last words, I felt like my body was warming up, I felt nauseous, and I puked. Arta instantly began scrubbing my face and clothing. I had no idea that any news from the past would have turned out this way.

Mother was advised to stop by Arta because onlookers were staring at us. Mother bid me farewell and stayed with Analia after I informed them that I needed to relax. I promised to talk to him as well and encouraged Mom not to give up; Arta escorted me to my flat.

After kissing me, she continued, "Don't worry about Mom and Dad; they will be fine; they are adults and they can work it out. Just focus on yourself; this is the greatest opportunity anyone can have. Enjoy it."

She was correct, but since they are my family, I can't just pretend that I don't feel anything. As far as I was aware, divorce was the last thing any lady in our tiny community was considering.

I entered the room, but I was upset or disappointed, so I sat on my bed and cried about what was happening to us. I also asked myself why we couldn't be together and why the smallest thing might separate us.

Mom had prepared some extra food, so I handed it to Ms. Marble since she had a larger refrigerator and could store it for me.

After performing a wash, I went to bed to say my prayers when I heard the phone ring. I wasn't shocked because so many people had been calling in the previous week asking for the housekeeper, so I picked up the phone and said, "She has moved from here. Call her on 332, please."

"Ariana, is that you? It's me Farhad," a man said abruptly.

I asked, "Sorry, who is this?" Because I was startled and needed some time to take it all in.

He inquired if I were free after repeating his name. "Can we converse for a little while?"

"Sure, why not," I immediately responded.

He continued, "It took me a week to figure out, how could I communicate with you, without creating any notice, I can clearly tell you I was pretty startled to see you in my class, and it felt wonderful at the same time."

He then waited for me to speak, saying, "I was glad to see a familiar face there too."

He then began inquiring as to how I came to be at that university and what had occurred to me. He also claimed to have seen Arta and my mother today, but he didn't approach them and say hello. He wasn't certain how my mother would handle it, which was very understandable.

He admitted, "This is my first year in the university as Master, I had studied in this place for more than six years till I obtained my PhD 1, and now I am actually lecturing." I replied all of his inquiries, and we talked about the subject he was instructing.

He was chuckling, something I had never heard of before because he rarely grins in class! At the conclusion of our talk, he wanted me to know that I could call him if I ever needed a friend, and I thanked him for the call.

After chatting to him, I completely forgot about how I felt earlier and felt relieved. He spoke in a professional and adult manner, and none of his statements hinted to anything in particular. He seemed like a really excellent image for me, in my opinion.

Chapter 26
Sunset Orange

Another week went by successfully, and I was settling into my surroundings and circumstances. I had to alert my year group leader when my father called to remind me of my doctor's appointment.

A car ride from the university to the hospital, which was about a two-hour journey away, was provided by the community of which I was a member and who are concerned with all women's rights (CCWR). Additionally, I was lucky enough to have free access to all the utilities.

I was feeling unwell on the way and had to puke. Since it was happening more frequently, I was prepared this time and carried a plastic bag around with me at all times. I also had a strong feeling that the meds I was taking were having a negative impact on my stomach. Or, something new to my list, I was experiencing motion sickness.

After visiting the expert and speaking with him, he made orders for a few tests, including an X-ray. I met my mother there. I had to take the examination and await the results.

When I asked her how she was doing, she replied, "Days are not passing for me easy since Arta is already gone and we had to admit Adam to rehabilitation center sooner than we planned, because he was getting worse day by day! He beat me two days ago for not giving him money to buy drugs."

She retrieved a tissue from her handbag to wipe away her tears before continuing, "Our divorce is final, and your father is now residing at the bakery. He claims that after Adam has left, he will begin looking for a rental space. I have started selling the remaining items in our and grandmother's home so that I can use the money I make to purchase a sewing machine and resume taking orders. I came up with the idea of producing various jams and selling them, if Rose will let me use her kitchen! Sitting around doing nothing will kill me."

Oh my God, there was a lot of bad news, but as Arta pointed out, I shouldn't worry about them because they are adults who can decide for themselves what they want to do. She could have easily closed her eyes to all the glitzy life and continued living with Dad as before, letting all of us be peaceful. Oh, Mother! Why couldn't you just be a regular homemaker and allow all of us be in harmony? Dad wasn't wealthy or schooled, but he was the father of your kids. I was thinking to myself.

I refrained from speaking since even a single word would have made me responsible for the entire scenario.

Perhaps it was best to be silent while she spoke, so I let her say whatever she wanted to say.

The nurse eventually arrived and asked us to go see the obstetrician for a checkup. Mother was told to stay out even though she wanted to attend.

I had never had an abdominal ultrasound performed by a doctor, so I didn't question why; otherwise, they would have explained that it was part of a standard examination.

Later, my mother was invited to participate as well. So, as I was lying on the bed, she requested my mother to sit beside me, repeated the ultrasound, turned up the volume and remarked, "I can hear a very strong heartbeat which is consequence of healthy fetuses!!!"

As I was processing what that meant, my mother abruptly dropped her handbag and yelled, "How can you be so sure about it?" Doctor presented her with a paper containing the blood test results that verified my pregnancy.

Mother was sobbing hard while holding her face.

The nurse helped me get dressed, the doctor wanted to see me alone, and then the head of the hospital joined us. I could hear my mother crying outside the door and battling to get in.

I suddenly experienced stomach pain, couldn't hold it back, and puked again. The doctor assisted me in cleaning up, calming down, and giving me some fresh juice. Once she saw that I was feeling a little better, she said, "You have morning sickness, and I can give you some tips to control it. I know you weren't aware of this, and also, I have been informed about your fiancé, what has he done to you and left you with a this! However, in the end, it is your body and your choice whether to have the child or not."

My cheeks began to warm up, I was concentrating on my shoes, and I was reluctant to glance at their faces.

"My dear, we are not here to judge you, we are here to help. You are a young girl who has just started university, and pregnancy and raising a child is a major matter and extremely expensive," the hospital's director remarked. "It's all up to you because, regrettably, your fiancé is still missing and the police are searching everywhere for him. Please wait before responding; you will be returning for a checkup the following week. You can let us know then."

Mother was waiting for me outside, but I had a hard time seeing her eyes because, evidently, she had been crying the entire time.

I was in a wheelchair, and security was stopping my mother from coming around me.

I was led to the orthopedist, who informed me that because I was pregnant, X-rays were no longer an option. Nevertheless, he wanted to take the cast off of my arm and leg and replace it with a flexible one, which would be much lighter and more manageable.

I didn't pay attention to him while he was speaking, then he added, "Ariana, I'm very sorry for what had happened to you; life has been so harsh lately. However, keep in mind that this exam is just another one like the others; try to pass it. I'll see you then; if you can, try to come over the weekend so that you don't require a quit any classes."

They were concerned that I would lose my balance as I wanted to walk and thanked him and the nurse. However, nothing happened. My thoughts were racing, and I completely forgot about my mother.

My mother was standing behind the same automobile that was still waiting when I heard my name and turned to see her. She smacked me and shouted, "I wanted you to make us proud, and this was what you offered us? Is there anything else you can do to make us look bad? I now understand what Adam meant when he claimed his friends were making fun of him because of your reputation." She afterwards departed in tears.

I sat in the car and started thinking back on what had occurred earlier the entire two hours of the trip.

She was correct, everything was my fault, and I knew it. I lacked the willpower to refuse anything! Neither to her nor to him. I am carrying the child of a man who tried to kill his own relative and wanted to kill me. Why did the worst thing start to happen when I thought I had control over everything and that the only thing I needed to focus on was myself and my future?

I walked out of the building happy and energized, but I returned feeling totally let down. I should still battle with the talents he left me even when he isn't here.

Chapter 27
Fuzzy Wuzzy Brown

The following day, I had class with Mr. Farhad. I really didn't want to see him, and I felt awful talking to even one of my classmates. What would they think of me if they found out I was pregnant?

The class lasted for more than three hours. There was a break for a half-hour, and since I felt more at ease after switching my cast, I thought of going to the canteen at that time.

When I left the classroom, Mr. Farhad was still there. He was gazing at me, and I believe he had noticed that my cast had changed. By staring at him, I felt something in my heart, but I disregarded it. Since my life was already chaotic, there was no time left for romance.

Talking with Elena made me think of Catherine because she was nice and gregarious, and she was one of the females in the class who was much closer to me than the rest.

She had pretty much told me everything about her life, but anytime she asked me a question about myself, I would try to avoid answering it and divert the conversation. She assumed I wasn't pleased to talk to her.

I didn't want anyone to know about my background or my family, and I wanted to get away from everyone and everything.

When Elena pointed out something that day, I was suddenly shocked to learn that she had been studying violin for three years with Mr. Zack as her instructor.

She also added that his classes had been suspended since someone hurt him a few weeks ago. She claimed that her cousin buried him alive after wanting to murder him.

My history wouldn't leave me alone and will eventually find its way back to me.

She informed me that his sessions will resume the next week and she encouraged me to go since the music might help my pains.

I hoped I could have talked to her in that same manner I used to talk to Catherine and asked for advice, but I couldn't!

I was the exception since I had a lot on my mind and the exam was the last thing I wanted to deal with. Everyone else was nervous because it was our first time and we had another, shorter class that day.

Ms. Marble had gone to see her daughter and was running late, so I didn't have to confront her. I needed some time to think. I found it quite difficult to make a decision. All I wanted was more time to think things through before I made a significant choice regarding the baby.

I considered walking to the nearest shop to buy some food because I was constantly hungry and there was nothing in the room.

I told the guard that it was becoming dark; he wanted to call the cap, but I opted to walk.

I don't know why I was scared, but a red automobile was following me! The driver of the car waved his shatters down and asked, "Do you need a ride?" I turned to look and noticed that it was Mr. Farhad.

I thanked him and explained that I needed a few groceries and had thought about getting some fresh air as well. I was irritated with myself for leaving my cabin.

He asked, "Are you okay? It will be quite impolite of me to just leave a lovely lady on the road without caring."

As usual, he gave me one of his endearing smiles and walked away when I said, "Everything's fine. Since I've decided to walk, it's a little tough for me but this what I need now."

I don't understand why it hurt to let him go. I genuinely wanted to be his girlfriend, but I knew that would be against the rules and that if he knew about my background or the kid I was expecting, he would despise me much more.

I returned as soon as I had done my shopping, had dinner, and was getting ready to do the wash when I heard phone call.

"Good night, Ariana. To see if you had found what you were looking for."

"Hello, Mr. Farhad, I've just finished eating, how are you doing?" I replied.

He continued talking about his father's relationship with my grandpa, mentioning how there are numerous pictures of the two of them in his home. He also mentioned how his father got married extremely late, making him the sole son he had by the time he was fifty.

His mother filed for divorce six months after his birth, and he hasn't heard from her since. He was raised by a nanny and has spent the most of his life with housemaids, and aides.

I did at least have a happy upbringing, especially with Catherine and my siblings. Despite the fact that I felt uncomfortable, he asked me to share more about Catherine's passing, so I did. He had the perfect listening ear, so I told him everything.

As we were conversing, a sharp pain in my uterus reminded me that I was still pregnant, and I began to question why I was speaking to another man while I was also pregnant. He was still wanting to talk if I didn't get out of the way.

Every time I would hear his voice, it would give me the energy I desperately needed. He was calm, kind, and very honest. Hearing how he paid his own way to college was fascinating. Perhaps this is why he cherished who he has become so highly.

I wanted to be myself and tell him everything, but I was afraid of losing a buddy once more.

I awoke screaming in the middle of the night from a terrible ache. I had a fever and noticed blood on my bedclothes, but I had no idea what to do.

I attempted to tidy up my bedsheet, changed, and returned, but this time I was unable to stand the pain and considered contacting a cap to get me emergency care.

Since there was no clinic open at that hour and I couldn't drive two hours to see my own doctor due to the noise, MS. Marble volunteered to accompany me to the hospital. We went to the emergency room at one of the city hospitals.

"They took me in, and after numerous examinations and tests, the doctor informed me that I had miscarried and that I would need to go to the operating room. Do you want to tell the father?" he asked.

Ms. Marble's lips also expanded wide, along with her eyes. I merely requested a brief period of time, and Ms. Marble inquired, "Does your family know about the baby? Is it his?"

I sobbed and covered my face as I informed her, "This is another gift he left for me. I found out about it yesterday while my mother was in the hospital with me. She smacked me and fled after hearing about the pregnancy."

"Oh, Ariana, seeing you in this state reminds me of my history. Please don't cry; this was God's decision to not let this child to come to this harsh world," she murmured as she approached and took me in her arms. "You are not to blame."

When the nurse returned and saw us sobbing, she told us not to worry since I am still young and could still become mother. She was confident that when the time was right, I would be holding my children in my arms.

Although my procedure didn't take long, I was urged to remain in the hospital for at least an additional hour.

Fortunately, I only had two classes the following day, and they were all in the afternoon. Ms. Marble assured me that she wouldn't speak to anyone as she drove away and that she would return to pick me up.

God has a plan for everything, I was thinking as I laid on the bed. He made a decision. I felt that my chest was no longer heavy, that I could breathe easily, that I was no longer feeling guilty, and I fell asleep.

Chapter 28
Banana Mania

Ms. Marble came to pick me up early so I could get to my lessons, and she assisted me in getting ready in my cabin. She was unsure whether or not I should enroll in classes because I was still experiencing dizziness from the surgery, but I argued that was the only option because I didn't want to mess anything up.

The subject was quite intriguing, the class was so packed that it was taking place in the hallway, there were two-year groups mixing, and I was feeling a little sleepy. I believe Elena also observed this. She brought us strong coffee during the break cause, according to her, she had some family difficulties last night and couldn't sleep at all. The coffee would assist us for a few hours.

During the break, my classmate Mohammed came and invited me to his birthday party, saying he had invited the entire class. I had always despised going to gatherings or festivities since I didn't want to make any promises. I thanked him and told him I would give it some thought because I still have trouble getting dressed or going somewhere.

"My mother is waiting to meet you. I've told her how courageous you've been, especially joining university after your accident and with all those injuries, he remarked. For my family, which is made up entirely of spoiled girls, seeing a girl like you—not to mention one who is both tall and attractive—is unique."

The way he was expressing himself especially made me chuckle, and I thanked him for the way he was thinking of me. Elena then joined the conversation and added, "Don't worry, I'll bring her along. As for her clothes and makeup, leave it to pros," while pointing to herself.

The second lesson was with Mr. Farhad, who I usually like seeing. I was trying to avoid looking at him directly since, for some reason that I don't understand, I was thinking about him so much.

I didn't want to get into another relationship at the time because I had just ended a terrible and unsatisfactory one.

After my lessons, I was so exhausted that I could barely feel my legs. Ms. Marble was not in her room, or else she would have come over as soon as she could.

My family was missing me, but I was frightened to phone them since I didn't know how my father would react if he discovered that I was pregnant.

I decided to call my father and chat with him as my heart was feeling particularly heavy and lonely at the time. I figured I would take a chance.

It was approximately eight o'clock in the evening, I knew Dad was in the bakery, and I used the public phone to contact him. Fortunately, he answered the phone when I said, "Dad, it's me Ariana, how are you, and why have you stopped calling me? Is now the appropriate time to speak?"

He appeared a little worn out and startled when he heard my voice. Oh Ariana, is that you? I didn't expect a call from you right now. How are things going? I assured him that I was only missing him and that my mother had not told him anything about me since she was more terrified of his reprimands than I was.

He informed me of their intention to divorce and stated, "I visit Adam every day. He has grown quite aggressive, and they have asked that I cease going there until he is stable."

I questioned him about the possibility of reconciliation, but he refused to even consider it, adding, "Our tale was ended, especially after she sold you for someone else's enjoyment! Please stop bringing up this topic in conversation with me because the Reena I married would never do such a crime."

I questioned him about his intentions and apologized for bringing up the past because I knew how exhausted he was. He said he was shortly moving to a studio apartment nearby, which is not ideal but will do until he sees Adam again. He advised me to focus on my studies and not to worry about him.

Nothing in the world can replace my parents, so I was delighted that I could finally speak with Dad. I knew we didn't get along well, but in the end, I needed my family members more than anything. I wished I could flip a magic wand to go back in time, erase the unpleasant memories, and only preserve the good ones. These dreams will never come true, as we all know, but I felt we could start anew if we could forgive one another.

I returned to the room and immediately had a shower despite being really exhausted and drowsy. By the time I was done, it was past midnight and there was still a lot to read!

The following day as I was leaving, I saw Ms. Marble was still gone. I asked a few other women working in the same building, and they told she had gone to stay with her daughter for a while because she is about to become a grandmother.

She seemed so youthful to me; it was difficult to believe she was going to become a grandma. It was interesting that she never addressed her daughter. She had already left her line to assist me, which I was grateful for, so I didn't mind at all. I prayed in my heart that her daughter would birth safely.

In Mr. Farhad's class, we were divided into several groups. He wanted us to collaborate, which was fantastic because none of us knew what we would encounter on the exam. He was trying to give us a hint and working in groups was making it much simpler. Everyone approved of his suggestions.

He was one of the university's youngest Masters, and other women in other departments were always attempting to connect with him. He was also much more attractive than when I initially met him at our house.

After a few days, I visited my orthopedic doctor again. Since he was aware of my abortion, he asked me to take an X-ray of my arm and leg. He was very pleased with the results, and after a few sessions of physiotherapy, my casts were entirely removed.

I ran into my dad that day as I was leaving the hospital. He was a little late, but he still made it. "Ariana, my girl, sorry for being late regrettably my car lift didn't show up and I was left seeking for a cap to drive me here, since it is far from where I reside," he said.

We walked to a neighboring restaurant for lunch after he gave me a big hug and I was overjoyed to see him. When he saw me in this state, he remarked, half of his anxieties vanished, and at least he can be confident I'll take care of myself. He appeared joyful but exhausted Dad informed me that my driver would no longer pick me up or drop me off; as a result, I would need to pay for all of my transportation going forward. Since Me Elsa vanished, they had been experiencing financial issues in the organization.

I requested Arta's number from my father, who also handed me some cash and advised me to dress appropriately going forward because all of my wardrobe options are only appropriate for parties. He was indeed correct; none of my clothing was suitable for a university setting.

Once he is settled in his new location, he stated he will attempt to visit more frequently.

Chapter 29
Shocking Pink

The midterm tests had already begun, and I was doing everything I could to keep up with everyone else by studying every evening after class.

Mr. Farhad called me virtually every evening, and we talked about a wide range of topics, particularly the themes we were studying in class. He was a great assistance. He claimed to have contacted my mother and told her they could stay in the house for however long they desired, but she had already informed him the house was unoccupied and he could obtain the key whenever he desired.

One of the smartest things I've ever said to someone was when I asked him to avoid merging our relationship with his work with my family. It was true that I didn't want to keep telling him things; it wasn't at all essential.

After a month, Ms. Marble returned at last. She was overjoyed and couldn't stop gushing about her grandson. For the entire dorm, she brought Donatus!

When my mother found out that Arta was having a girl, I can still picture how devastated she was.

It was like a century ago in our small village when women who gave birth to their husband's son received greater respect from the other.

For a few weeks, my mother hadn't given me any updates, and when I tried to call home, no one was picking up because everyone had already left. Although chatting to folks in that house was the last item on my bucket list, I remembered she had planned to stay with Aunt Rose.

Since I didn't want to talk to anyone in that home, I finally requested Ms. Marble to phone Rose and ask for my mother one night. No one could have understood it better than Ms. Marble!

After taking the call and asking a ton of questions, Rika called my mother. "Hi, it's me Ariana, and I wanted to call you since I was missing you. I know you despise me a lot. If you'd want, I can cut the line."

"How are you, I was missing you too. I was ashamed of myself, especially after hurting you that day. I know it wasn't your fault," she said after I overheard her sobbing. I was hoping you'd call me soon and accept my apology.

She was pretending I was Arta and kept enquiring about the baby, so I was overjoyed to hear all those things, but the one thing she still didn't know was about the miscarriage!

I informed her I had miscarriage a day after we met and then detailed everything because I knew she was surrounded by her sister and relatives.

She seemed relieved after hearing it, in my opinion. She claimed that they had launched a small catering company and were also receiving orders from outside sources. Rose and Rika were also assisting her. She also said that she would visit me shortly.

Hearing her speak was pleasant; I saw that she seemed more assured this time, and it was excellent that she had been able to escape her past.

Though I wished I could, where was my home? Arta once told me that if I had a lengthy vacation, I could join her.

She was claiming that Benjamin is content there and that he earns a nice wage in addition to receiving a lot of respect for holding a job. She was eager to obtain a loan to purchase their own home, but I suppose it was premature, it was still their choice.

After the tests, Mohammed's birthday celebration was held, and everyone eagerly anticipated it. I was hesitant to leave. Despite Elena's persistent pestering, I continued to say no. Sadly, I had to learn how to be tough the hard way this time.

Since I knew what to expect at these parties, I honestly stopped finding it fascinating.

Mr. Farhad was also invited to the party, but as a teacher, he was not permitted to attend any solitary gatherings or to approach any of the students so closely! He was a good man, but he was getting so near to me that I knew there were many other ladies waiting for this chance than me.

More than losing my seat, I was worried about what the institution would think. He was relieved to hear that I was not joining the party, therefore I was doing my best to keep a barrier between us. I believe that increased his liking of me, though I'm not sure why.

The night of the party, I also considered leaving, so I asked Ms. Marble to point out a few stores where I might find some clothing for myself.

I also learned how to travel to those locations via public transit. Farhad wished to accompany me, but I declined since I didn't want to be seen with him. The distance between the town center and our university was twenty minutes.

Ms. Marble provided me the location of a mall that was less expensive but more than adequate and was located closer to us than the others.

I visited a few stores since I needed the money and thought their pricing were better than the others. I didn't want to spend a lot of money, so I bought a few.

While exploring, I came upon a sizable bookshop. I decided to check inside, and there was a sitting place where I could take some of those books and read them more thoroughly in quiet.

I was looking at the novels when someone else sat down in front of me. When I looked up, it was Zack!

He told me to calm down because there were people observing us when I recognized him, but I became afraid. He appeared to have followed me to the store after seeing me in the mall.

As Edwin informed me, he had urged you to get involved but somehow drag me to his hook, but you had defied him and you had to pay for it. "I know seeing me will bring back your horrible memories, but I needed to thank you for saving my life by putting yourself in risk."

I struggled mightily to keep my emotions under control as I informed him, "I did what any normal human will do. I couldn't allow him to hurt you. As you said, he was mentally ill, and I didn't realize that until it became a threat to my and other people's lives."

Since he was confident Edwin would return to finish what he had begun, he was quite upset that the police had not yet been able to apprehend him. For this reason, he had planned to leave the nation and relocate to a location where he would be difficult to trace.

He warned me to take precautions as well, although he didn't want to stay for very long. His face was completely destroyed, and there was a massive scar beneath each of his eyes that appeared to have been badly slashed. He said that he spent eight hours in that grave!

He went, but I remained motionless, simply believing that I was in the past and that Edwin would come and slap me for talking to his cousin. As I looked at my hands and noticed the books, I was immediately reminded of where I was.

Even on the way home, I was frightened by my own shadow as the light abruptly vanished! I had the impression that someone was looking out for me as I went to my cabin.

I was trying to open the door to my room when Ms. Marble walked out and said hello. I was really startled and yelled really loudly. She was astonished to see me in that condition, questioned my well-being, and assumed I had been punched since I had nothing with me.

She led me into her room, gave me a glass of water, and then inquired as to what had transpired. I told her what happened, and she immediately notified mall security that my handbag and shopping bags had gone missing from the bookstore. He assured us that we would get them back.

After a while, the past will be history, Ms. Marble advised, so focus on the future instead. She was making an effort to assist me. Also suggested I speak with a phycologist to obtain advice on overcoming my phobias.

I informed her that I really couldn't afford it, but she had a plan for that as well. She mentioned that her daughter is a dentist who works in a clinic with a counseling psychologist, and she will ask her to speak with her about her fees. She also mentioned that the same person attends the Church twice a week and provides free consultations for anyone in need.

I hoped that would distract me for a while. Since my family was already in a mess, I didn't want to engage them this time. I suppose that was sufficient for them. I wished to solve my issues on my own so that I can regain the self-confidence that had been taken from me.

Chapter 30
Pink Flamingo

Good thing we were leaving in a secure community since my groceries and handbag were located and returned to me the next day!

I made the decision to seek counseling after that, and I first encountered Doctor Lili at a church. We were introduced to one another by Ms. Marble. She was willing to assist me without charging me, even though Dr. Lili appeared to be considerably older than her.

I was really fortunate to have Ms. Marble in my life; she was a compassionate woman who did her best to look out for me as her daughter.

I began a few sessions with Lili, but she never inquired about my background or what had happened to me; instead, I just discussed my schoolwork, my time at school, my classmates, and Farhad because I needed to tell someone that I was speaking with him.

I asked her not to tell anyone about it because if they found out, one of us would be asked to leave. She claimed that she was responsible for keeping all of my secrets safe and that she wouldn't discuss anything outside of this room with anyone.

I tried my best, but I wasn't yet ready to speak about my history since I didn't want to remember even the most basic details about my family. She was attempting to broach various topics, and perhaps there was a way to do so, but I was also aware of what was occurring and was taking precautions to prevent it.

She urged me to go see my family and make an effort to spend some time with them, saying that while it would be impossible to reunite them all in one location, I could continue to see each of them separately.

Nearing the holiday season, practically everyone left the dorm. Ms. Marble was going to spend time with her grandson, and I was requested to go as well since there was no place available for breaktime.

I asked my father if it was okay and then I spent some time with him. He was pleased that I had chosen to be with him rather than my mother and he also mentioned there were many things he would like to share with me.

Mr. Farhad offered to spend some time getting to know me because he was lonely and had no plans, but I declined and gave many justifications about how my family was expecting me.

I'm not sure what he anticipated, but there have been occasions when I wish I had never met him. After everything I had gone through, I had no room in my heart for love of anyone.

Dad's house was too small, but I suppose it was adequate for him. Everything, including the kitchen, hallway, bedroom, and bathroom, were in a row without walls, with the exception of the bathroom. I suppose this was how a studio apartment should be laid out.

Dad's appearance changed, and I got the impression that he was waiting to talk to me. When the time came, he said, "I have met someone, she is a compassionate, very kind and charitable, after dating her for a few times, I have asked her to marry me and she has accepted, soon I will be moving to her location."

I'm not sure why I wasn't expecting to hear it, but it was entirely acceptable and within his legal rights, so I was a little taken aback.

"Dad, what about Mom?" without thinking, I questioned.

He grew irritated and remarked, "What about Mom? Why do you say that? Did she ever consider me during those times when she was getting dressed up and going to all the events in the city without her husband? Was I ever invited to one of those locations by her? You're asking what about her, but she treated me like no one or a cash machine. I finally would like to feel alive once more."

I instantly apologized, saying that I shouldn't have ruined his happiness and that I should have let him live his life as he had desired.

He approached me as I was sitting down and said, "Ariana, you are the only one who can understand, how tough it is to be locked in a relationship, you know quite well how much I battled, how much I fought with your mother."

He wiped away his tears and added, "As a man, my wife didn't want me anymore, as a father I had lost my value in the family, three of you were out of my sight, no one needed me. We made a tremendous mistake getting married, and the bigger mistake was continuing it while I've been lonely for so long."

"I didn't object when your mother suggested having more children since it would strengthen the foundation of the relationship, but once the third child was born, the distance grew. Unless you don't have your own family first, you won't be able to understand how complex it is."

"Dad, I am sorry for my response; I was a little stunned and it slipped out that way. You have all the rights in the world to be pleased and no one can take that away from you, not even me. Live the way you want and no matter what, I will accompany you," I said while holding his hand.

In order for us to meet, he claimed he had invited her to join for lunch. I was reflecting on what he had said to me that day, which was actually true.

Mother, who'd already lost everything—her love, her husband, and her family—was regrettably preoccupied with me and focused on collecting a large sum of money so I could pave the way for the other family members.

I tried to appear normal. Dad was tense, so he repeatedly pleaded with me to act properly and refrain from saying anything that may offend her.

He answered the door, and to my surprise, Ms. Jane was my soon-to-be stepmother!

I welcomed her in and completely forgot about her relationship with my dad as she came forward to give me a hug. We discussed Ms. Marble, my lessons, and my cabin.

She added that she had been chosen to lead CCWR (Community Care of Women Rights) and that she was doing her very best to look after the females who needed it. She also offered me a job, saying that I could start earning money while I was still in school. I thought her concept was good.

I was overjoyed when I realized who my father would eventually settle down with. She was a woman who would undoubtedly heal my father's old wounds. She aided in my transportation to the university where she made Ms. Elsa sign all of my paperwork. How am I going to refuse her? She was ideal for my father.

I made the decision to go earlier than I had intended, I believed they looked amazing next to one another.

Ms. Jane merely said, "Ariana, please don't get me misunderstood, you have the right to know more than the rest," when asked about her connection with my father that day.

"He called me one night, and because I assumed it was about you and I was too concerned, I asked him over to my house.

"He was trembling and bawling uncontrollably. I don't know if any of them mentioned it to you earlier, but your mom, dad, and I went to the same school. That night, he began to talk about his relationship with your mother, your grandmother's desire before she passed away, and the toxic relationship between you and Ms. Elsa's son.

"He was confused and mystified; I attempted to help him, but every time he tried to reach out to your mother, she turned him away. One night, he even had suicide thoughts; if I had not arrived at the scene sooner, he would not have survived. This is how things began. It was definitely not beautiful."

Since both of them had negative relationships in the past, I kissed her and wished them a happy and prosperous marriage. However, in my heart, I wished my mother had been there instead of her since she was sorry for what she had done and could have tried again with him.

Chapter 31
Caribbean Green

Before I went, Dad had requested me to let Mom and Arta know about his plans. I didn't want to continually be the bearer of bad news.

I also, absolutely forgot to inquire about Adam's health. Since Mom was living with them, there was no way to avoid encountering them when I went to Aunt Rose's house as my next stop. As soon as I arrived, I was hesitant to ring the bell since I wished there was another option to see Mother and spend some time with her without being disturbed by my aunt and her family.

I rang the doorbell, and Mr. Neal (Aunt Rose's husband) answered. Luckily, Rose and Rika had left for a ceremony, I was just too delighted not to see them!

With a list in her hand, a mask, gloves, and a hair net on, Mom appeared busy. I went over to her and gave her a hug as I was really missing her. She was in the kitchen packaging meal for delivery. She invited me to the table, served me one of her best beef and beans meals, and sat next to me since she was overjoyed and clearly awaiting me.

She was already aware of my travel plans and the fact that I had visited my father first, but she persisted in asking me various questions to learn more about him and how he was doing.

She could be better off hearing about father's remarriage through Arta.

With the money she has been saving up, she stated she plans to rent her own home very soon. She also mentioned receiving a job offer to work as a full-time chef at a restaurant.

She was making sensible decisions, and my eyes were awakened to the realities of life. It appeared that she was uncomfortable living with her own sister. I reassured her that taking this move is a positive one and that perhaps in the future, as she expands her network and gains experience, she will discover something greater.

She also added that Mr. Farhad's attorney had contacted to let her know she could stay in the house as long as she wanted without even having to pay rent! She did thank them, though, and said it was too late to show kindness.

He never stated that he was going to call my mother. Perhaps after talking to me, he began to sense something and attempted to capture my sympathy by doing that, but the most important thing is that he doesn't realize that I no longer have a heart or a family!

"Ariana, you look mature and more attractive. The subject you are studying at the university is truly a good fit for your character," Mr. Neal said as he joined us at the table. Then he again complimented me and said that he hoped Rika would one day have the courage to consider her future clearly rather than playing and partying nonstop.

After all, my intention was only to spend one night there. Mom was too exhausted after dinner, so I reasoned that going to bed early would be a good way to avoid my aunt and her daughter.

She brought a mattress for me as well because she was sleeping on the floor in their guest room.

I prayed for my mother at night while holding her hand and wished her a prosperous future. I was concerned about what would happen to her if she discovered about my father and Ms. Jane.

Dad had bought me a bus ticket to the south for the following day. I had to depart early in order to arrive on time. Mother handed me some sandwiches to eat on the road.

She remarked, "I'm pleased for your dad, I'm sure that witch after all will offer him everything I didn't," before walking away. My mouth dropped open because I couldn't believe she was so at ease while speaking all of those sentences! She was constantly reacting so strongly to her that seeing her so composed was odd.

I questioned her, "How did you hear about this? I've seen her so often in your father's bakery.

"When I discovered she was having a date with your dad in one of the best restaurants after I had followed her from school, I was initially furious and wanted to assault her, but I restrained myself.

"After giving it some serious thought, I realized that she is a nice woman and that losing your father was my fault; she had nothing to do with it—after all, she was the one who rescued your future.

"I know what I have done, I can't blame anyone for it, my wonderful family and kids are all gone," she stated after wiping away her tears.

Although it was difficult to say goodbye, I suppose that was the ideal time to leave before Rose and Rika woke up!

I assured her that I would ask Arta to phone and notify immediately I arrived.

The things that were happening one after another in my family were more than usual, and it was too much to process at once.

I was early for the bus. I was fortunate enough to have an empty seat next to me on the bus, which allowed me to comfortably extend my legs and nap.

I enjoyed the weather once I got off the bus and saw Arta waiting for me at the station; she looked so joyful and chubby! It took us long to get to her house.

After all the embraces and kisses, she said, "Oh Ariana, I have a lot to share and show you, I am so excited you are here, you are the first person from back home, is visiting us. Having a family member is very pleasant."

I couldn't wait to hold my darling, pudgy Analia and couldn't wait to see her home.

Their home was close to the river, a short distance from the city and surrounded by other identical-looking residences. She had a larger garden and faced the river, which was the sole positive aspect.

Analia was even more adorable because she was plump and had curly hair all over her.

I was relieved to see a bed in the room I was supposed to share with Analia because I no longer needed to sleep on the floor. Two bedrooms were located on the second level of the home, which also had a hall and kitchen.

The garden had a great view, and it was simple to access the river, which was a little frightening, especially for young children.

Benjamin was at work; Arta remarked that he usually returned in the evening; it appeared that now that he had been promoted, his time had improved!

We had some time to talk before Analia went to bed. "I know it's too soon, but I'm expecting," Arta remarked.

I jumped out of my seat when I heard it, saying, "Oh that means another chubby baby, I love it, congrats sister." I was so thrilled.

"Benjamin is a bit afraid how we are going to sustain two kids in the future," she added, flushing red and touching her belly. "Sometimes he is so excited, and other times he is simply unhappy."

According to Grandmother, "Every time a new baby would join our family, it will be a blessing," I informed her.

She began enquiring about our parents, and I realized that she wasn't aware of any current developments. I assumed that it was my responsibility to inform her.

I made an effort to avoid sounding odd as I began to explain how my parents did not get along, how much they fought, and numerous other instances from the past, before ultimately telling her about my dad's marriage.

She was initially shocked, but after I revealed who he was marrying, she was delighted, saying, "I like Ms. Jane, not only since she was my principal, but mostly because of her charisma. I hope Mother will be okay with it. She is a very strong woman, and I am sure Dad has a lot to learn from her."

I told her that my mother had been informed of it before any of us and that I was hoping Ms. Jane could keep him content.

She grabbed my hand and asked, "Ariana, what's going on with our family? Why can't they get along? What about Adam, the poor guy? What lies ahead for him?"

She started crying after that, so I quickly changed the conversation and began asking her about her pregnancy, the baby shopping, and other things to try and get her to shift her mind.

When Benjamin did arrive, we chatted about my education and the subjects that I was taking and he left without eating dinner.

Since he is so busy, Arta claimed he rarely eats at home. He is actually eating in the workplace.

Chapter 32
Neon Carrot

My vacation was still a week away, and I was already boarded at Arta's place, with nothing to do!

She was busy doing housework and cooking all day, while I kept Analia occupied.

I planned to go to town one day, but Arta was not in the mood and Analia was too tired to accompany me, so I went alone. I walked half of the distance and then took the bus the rest of the way.

The weather was perfect, Arta gave me the names of a few places that I should check out.

I was dressed differently from the natives, and it was evident that I was a stranger. The odd thing was, in every shop where I wanted to buy something, I had the same problem: the price!

They were keep changing the price of one item, by the time I was reaching to the counter, it was increased ten percent!

I didn't mind at all; I knew they hardly had a customer so I could understand how hard was to manage a day.

That day, I had a lot of fun by myself; I went to practically every business and talked to everyone; I realized how much I had changed and how socialized I had gotten, which was an excellent thing when compared to a few months previously!

I was too preoccupied to notice; I had been away all day. Arta requested me to take her smartphone, but I was unfamiliar with it, so I simply left it and returned. Anyone with a cellphone in my time came from an affluent family.

I decided to walk back home, on my way I thought of buying a small doll for Analia. As I was paying, I noticed Benjamin enter the shop while holding the hand of another lady!

He didn't notice my presence at first, but as the cashier began speaking with me, he recognized my voice and turned to see who it belonged to…

After noticing me, he dropped the lady's hand and began speaking in a formal manner, as if they were merely colleagues; nevertheless, we both knew what was going on, and the lady became irritated and said, "Benji, what happened to you, sweetheart, as if you saw a ghost?"

I hurriedly exited the store, unsure how to react, and simply began walking. He rapidly pursued me and shouted for me to stop walking so he could explain.

I told him he didn't have to explain anything because it was between him and Arta, but he insisted.

He said, "Let's sit on one of the benches," and then went on to say, "Arta is pregnant, and I'm having a hard time talking to her because she's so stressed out about everything. I know it's too early to have a second child, so I asked her if she didn't want to keep it, and let's do something about it before it's too late."

Then he took a handkerchief from his pocket and wiped his brow sweetly before continuing, "I was also concerned about how I would feed my family if I lost my job?

"My manager, Lili, invited me to supper one night, and we became very close friends after that.

"She recently divorced and was looking for a friend to talk to; now that my eyes have been opened, I can clearly see that she is expecting more than a friendship from me, and I am so afraid to say no and break up with her; she is my manager; she has increased my salary and given me a new position; it is too easy for her to fire me."

"I can't afford another work; right now, we have a house, a car, and money; with a second baby, our expenses will skyrocket; what will happen if I leave?"

"Ariana, I'm sorry about everything, but now that my family has a home and the riches, they've always desired, can you tell me how to erase all of this?"

Why wasn't I astonished by his story? Because it was so similar to mine: keeping people happy by providing them what they want while ignoring the future!!!

When I inquired if they had any sort of physical interaction, he replied no, but she has been pushing for it, and he is the one who is rejecting because he isn't ready yet!

I had no choice but to trust him at the time. I had an idea while sitting there and informed him about it. He wasn't sure whether it would work, but there was no harm in trying!

I arrived home earlier than he did, and I promised him I wouldn't tell her about what I witnessed. Arta was a little concerned as to why I was late, but when she saw the shopping bags in my hand, she calmed down and commented, "Someone has truly gone to town."

Then I presented her the beautiful silk shawl that I had gotten her, as well as the doll to young Analia, and they were both ecstatic.

Benjamin arrived a little later, and this time he sat at the table with us for supper, scrubbed the dishes, and served tea for all of us after dinner, saying, "Arta, my manager Lili has been so wonderful to our family, I think we owe her at least a dinner in our place."

"Why not," Arta said with a smile, "it's actually a fantastic time to invite her, because Ariana is here and can be a tremendous help."

I smiled at them and answered, "Why not, anything for my sister?" before turning to face Benjamin.

"There won't be much, not more than five," Benjamin said when Arta inquired about how many guests we were expecting and if she needed to borrow some extra chairs from the neighbors. "I was only planning on inviting my manager, her secretary, and her accountants."

That night, I had a different concept about what was going to happen; in fact, I was the one who came up with the idea of inviting her. I was hoping that once she saw Arta and Analia, she would alter her mind, but I wasn't sure! I was terrified that Arta would find out about their relationship!

The entire night was spent in prayer.

Chapter 33
Mountain Meadow

I requested Arta to let me do all the cleaning and arranging because I needed to burn some extra fats. The party was in two days and there was a lot to do in the house.

She also wanted me to go into town and pick out a dress for her because none of her old ones fit her.

I tried to calm Benjamin down by telling him, "If you want this to succeed, you need to trust me, as well as your feelings for your wife and child; this is the only way we can finish the relationship without you losing anything. So let us pray and be hopeful."

I'm not sure what more to say. Instead of someone soothing me down, I was calming him!

Arta prepared three different courses, while I prepared some sides and desserts. I instructed her to attempt to go closer to Benjamin's boss and be more cordial, knowing full well that this would make Lili uncomfortable, which was exactly what I was hoping for.

There was no way I could let her ruin this lovely family!

That night, she arrived later than everyone else, and I was worried that she had changed her mind and wouldn't show up, but she did. Benjamin was so tense that he forgot to greet her.

Arta walked up to the front and introduced herself, then invited her in. I introduced myself too, after, took her to where others were seated. There was a total of five individuals, two females and the rest were men.

Analia was the show's star; she was holding the doll I gave her and showing it off to everyone; she even sat in Lili's lab.

Arta delivered drinks for everyone, and Lili inquired, "Oh, my dear, why didn't you serve yourself? It's really disrespectful that we drink without the host."

"You are really sweet," she replied with a smile, "fortunately, I'm expecting so, I can't join you for drink, but I will absolutely serve myself first for meal."

Lili's face flushed as everyone praised Benjamin; she looked surprised but couldn't disguise it, so she questioned Arta in hushed tones, "How much more to go?"

"Another seven months, I imagine!" Arta replied, touching her belly.

Lili finished her drink and inquired if she may have another. I purred for her right away. I believe she was calculating how long she had known Benjamin in comparison to the fetal age in her head!

After a little while, the dinner was served, and everyone was talking about work and the office. Lili was irritated, and she spent the rest of the night avoiding Benjamin.

Arta invited Lili to come view the garden and listen to the river, so they both strolled to the rear garden, and I was busy clearing up the dinner table like it was back in the day!

Benjamin walked into the kitchen and begged me to keep an eye on Arta so Lili wouldn't harm her.

I hurriedly left everything in the kitchen and joined them outside; the other lady was Lili's secretary, and she accompanied me outside as well.

They were both sitting and talking about nature when I asked if they needed anything. Lili thanked me and invited me to sit alongside her, where she then began to inquire about my university.

I began by discussing my subjects and classes to her, as well as telling her about one of our masters who was more enjoyable than the others (Mr. Farhad).

She strikes me as a mature and understanding woman; I'm not sure why Benjamin was so afraid of her or why she was interested in him; there were so many other alternatives for her outside; what did she see in him? Love is blind, and it was blindly blind in their instance!

That night came to an end sooner than we expected, and Lili was the first to leave, thanking Arta for allowing her to visit her house and family; Arta also informed her that she is extremely lonely here and that having a friend like her is very important.

Benjamin took Analia to bed as Arta and I started cleaning up. Arta was overjoyed to have met Lili, yet something was bothering her. She inquired whether I felt the same way, and I told her that all of these feelings were caused by pregnant hormones.

I was so exhausted that night that I went to bed without changing my clothing.

I was sure something was wrong when Benjamin stopped talking to any of us, tried to hide himself in the office, and came home so late for a few days.

He finally decided to take me to town on the last day of my stay and show me around. Arta wasn't able to join us because she was suffering from morning sickness and couldn't stay in the car for lengthy periods of time.

Benjamin came to a halt near a coffee shop, and we both got out. He then informed me that there is someone who wanted to meet me before I depart.

When I walked in, I was greeted by Lili, who stood up and walked to the front, shook my hand, and invited me to her table, after which Benjamin left us alone.

I wasn't expecting it, but I tried to be cool and grin the entire time.

"I asked Benjamin to invite you here because I wanted to meet you alone, and you planned the entire invitation?" Then she took a sip of her coffee and continued, "I knew it after talking with you in the Garden before I left that night."

"I praised your effort in assisting your sister's marriage because it was a clever strategy. I just wanted to let you know that I received your message and that I will take a step back from their lives. Don't worry, I will not harm Benjamin or his family. I will undoubtedly continue to help them, especially now, when Arta requires my assistance."

I was almost in tears as I told her how delighted I was that she took it positively and what a wonderful woman she was. I apologized if we had inadvertently wounded her in any way.

"I met Benjamin the day after my divorce, I was so dispersed and dissatisfied, I was carrying so much, angry as ever with myself, and the only person available was Benjamin," she added with a smile. "I wasn't really thinking.

"I was crazy for days following that night for everything, but after a while, my eyes opened to what I was doing, and I appreciate you helping me stop."

"Lili, my beloved, I'm sorry, but you deserve better than Benjamin, and there will undoubtedly be someone out there for you, who loves you for who you are, not for how much money you have."

I drank a sip of water to clear my throat, and continued, "My family has gone through a lot for the last year we have lost a lot of things, I have been the cussed of most of them only because I wanted to go to university and was not willing to marry. I hope you understand that this was the tiniest thing I could do for my sister to at least keep her family safe."

"Anywhere in the nation you have stock, call me, I have contacts," she added as she slapped her hand and said bravo. She then handed me her business card and said, "Anywhere in the country you have stock, call me, I have contacts."

I sat for a while before Benjamin arrived and we both went.

He was overjoyed and began thanking me, saying that now he can sleep soundly at night without worrying about the next day.

It was difficult to say goodbye, especially to Analia, who was the cutest creature on the planet. Arta had already prepared my lunch for me to eat on the way.

Arta assured me that the next time I visit, I will undoubtedly meet the new baby. I was going to miss them all, but it was time for me to depart.

My ticket was for 2:00 p.m., and I was already fatigued as I walked to the bus, wondering, as I had done the previous time, that I could locate an empty seat and rest a little.

What a wonderful holiday I had; there was nothing but pleasant news. One last item on my to-do list was to pay a visit to Adam…But, as he was still not settled and couldn't accept new Ariana, I believe I should postpone it to another time.

Chapter 34
Outer Space

I overslept on the bus and realized it two stations later, which was too late. I got down and it was too dark to figure out where I was, so I asked a couple individuals and found out.

The taxi station was about to close, so I waited for half an hour until a taxi arrived, driven by a man with a long beard and specs. I told him what had happened and requested if he could drop me off in front of my hostel; he initially refused, but after I assured him I would pay more than the cost, he agreed.

I was thinking to myself that I needed to get a job and save some money so that I could purchase a cellphone. I was too hungry, and I was looking for the food Arta had prepared for me, but I remembered it was in the back of the car, and I didn't want him to stop on the way, and I was concerned they wouldn't let me in because I was late.

The driver offered me some cookies, and I figured if I declined, he'd feel horrible, so I took two and thanked him; as he said, his daughter is the one who constantly bakes and packs the cookies for him.

I was feeling so drowsy that I didn't mind closing my eyes for a moment, as the driver indicated it would take almost an hour to get there.

I felt someone was petting What kind of dream was I having when I sensed someone petting my head and felt his lips on my hand? Who was he, exactly? It wouldn't surprise me if it was Farhad, as I've been thinking about him a lot lately!

I smiled as I opened my eyes and found myself in his embrace! Is it possible that I'm dreaming? To ensure that I would wake up, I slapped my face.

"Welcome back, my love, like I had promised you, wherever you go, this bond is unbreakable, baby," he added with a giggle as he stood in front of me, pointing to my eyes and holding my hand.

My mouth was still shut, and I was wishing in my heart that this was only a foolish dream, or a nightmarish nightmare, that I could wake up and everything would be fine, but no, he was there, and my baggage were just by me.

He was more repulsive than ever. Edwin, my cursed love has returned!

I returned to his old family home, where, shockingly, the police had no control and the property should have been shuttered. Everything was the same as previously, with the identical sofa, tea table, and even my nightgown waiting for me on the bed.

I was wondering what I should do if all of them were true. Will I play the sweet and loving fiancée and let him do anything he wants with me? Is it okay if I dress up as a doll and dance? Do you want me to be his Scolari maid? Or will I have to battle for my life? I was still trying to make sense of the situation.

I smiled and let him abuse me anyway he pleased! I didn't want to fight this time; instead, I wanted to return whatever he had given me! I was always planning for this day in my lonely corner; I knew he would return, but I didn't know when.

I wasn't afraid of him anymore, but I didn't want to get caught up in his antics, so I gave myself some time to ponder and didn't rush things.

I asked where he had been all this time and he claimed he had surprises for me.

"The ideal location to conceal it was in your house; no one would suspect I was hiding there. I had been sleeping in your room all this time, precisely where your bed used to be, the room was smelling like you, and I could see you everywhere!" he responded.

How did you come across me? I inquired. "I never lost you, I was just not revealing myself to anyone, that didn't mean I wasn't there, I was following you around everywhere, I knew they wouldn't let you stay for your holidays, so that's when I started scheming how to get to you, and here we are, back together like love birds." He was giggling and said something.

I inquired as to where his mother was, and he replied that she was also present; we would meet her soon, but first he wanted me to change into my red night gown.

While changing in the room, I was thinking that if Ms. Elsa was also present, my work would be made more difficult; I had not expected to see her.

I put on a lot of make-up and put on the perfume that was driving him insane; he was in tears when he saw me like that. walked up to me and kissed me, then began walking with my hand in his.

He brought me to one of his grandfather's chambers, which I hadn't been allowed to view previously. The space was larger than my entire house, so he instructed me to close my eyes and then carefully open them in front of the wall, making sure I didn't miss anything.

There was a large wall in front of me with images of my grandmother from the moment she was choked to death, as well as all of his steps. Catherine's images, her eyes, and her body were all on display.

He was the one who put them to death…

My grandmother's murderer had been by my side the entire time…my dearest friend had died for me…

But I wasn't weeping anymore; my voice had died inside of me, and he was astonished to see me without a response. On the table was a box containing all of my grandmother's missing jewels. I remember how hard my mother and aunt Rose searched for it.

On the lower side of the wall, there were images of Zack, the poor boy, and the place where he had been buried; I still remember how they got him out of there. I didn't know if he realized he was still alive!

His eyes twinkled like diamonds, as if he expected me to start shouting and begging for my freedom at any minute, but I was still in a trance.

He glanced at me and asked, "Why aren't you astonished to see all of this? Your fiancé had gone to great lengths to get to you, and then you had left me so graciously!"

"I knew it, and it was nothing new to me," I continued, "but I kept my tongue shut because I wanted you so much." He kissed my hand and whispered in my ear that I had become wiser during my absence from him.

In the corner of the room, there were two hospital beds, one of which had a lady sleeping on it; I couldn't see her face because it was covered in white bandages. Who might that be, I wondered? Only one eye was visible.

I didn't want to go any further, but he grabbed my hand and said, "Come on, darling, it's very impolite not to say hello to your mother-in-law."

Oh, my goodness, did I hear him correctly? What exactly has he done to his mother? Ms. Elsa, how sad! She tried to say something, but Edwin stopped her and continued, "It was all her fault, she wanted to force me to go back to France and leave you alone, but you were carrying my child, I was finally going to be a father, how could I leave? That day, the only thing that sprang to mind was to splatter acid on her face in the hopes that she would stop bothering me and leave me and my fiancé alone!"

I was terrified, but I was trying to keep my emotions in check, especially when I saw his mother on the bed!

"My love, I am sorry for the baby, the doctor said it was not your fault, all those medicines you were using caused us to lose our baby, but he also said we can keep trying and for sure I am not giving up to become a parent, sadly I had to finish your doctor, because he was going to report to the police, but don't worry at all this time, I have gathered all the information we need!"

I felt sick to my stomach, my body shivered, and I couldn't think of a way to aid his mother. I hadn't expected her to show up.

"I want you to sit and drink with me like in the old days," he added, bringing two wine glasses and asking me to accept one.

I was the good girl, and I drank the whole thing, knowing it was mixed with something because of the taste. My head was starting to feel heavy, so I dropped the glass and fell to the ground.

Chapter 35
Radical Red

I awoke with a discomfort in my neck, was unable to move my arm, and my legs were tethered to the bed; Ms. Elsa was also present.

"Did you have a decent slumber, sorry I had to sedate you, because the treatment I was intending to conduct was a bit painful, I couldn't see you struggling!" Edwin exclaimed when he spotted me moving.

I inquired, "What have you done to me this time?"

He kissed my lips and added, "I branded you with my name, or let's say I labeled you with my name, on the neck, so that whenever you look in the mirror, you will remember me and know who you belong to."

I couldn't believe what I saw as he held the mirror in front of me; he was right…

I had a large cut around my neck, and I could clearly see his name.

Ms. Elsa was attempting to say something, but her voice was distorted, and all I heard was, "Edwin, you will burn in hell, Edwin, all those people you have killed and wounded up to this point, their souls are waiting to avenge you."

He approached her and struck her in the stomach, saying, "Shot up, don't make me burn your other eye, do you know why I haven't murdered you yet, I wanted you to struggle, and every minute you wonder yourself why you introduced me to Ariana?

"You knew I was sick, you knew I'd murdered my first French lover in Paris, but you wanted me to keep going. It's all your fault; I wanted to commit suicide, but you told me to start afresh, so be quiet and watch.

"You told me their family is cheap and useless; they don't have anything to lose, or if they do, it won't bother them; we can shut their mouths with our money, especially her mother."

He began to cry heavily and added, "I told you Ariana is pregnant, I am going to be a dad, instead of feeling glad for me, what did you do?" The first words out of your mouth were, "How could I be so sure the baby was mine? You told me to leave her behind and flee away, as we usually did, to start over in another country."

Then he kept punching her in the head, despite my pleas for him to stop, and he left the room a few minutes later. No voice could be heard coming from that rapped-up body…I kept calling her. Sadly, there was no response…

I reasoned that it was now or never, and I needed to do something before he returned. I looked about to see what I could find, and there was an IV stand beside me!

I paused for a moment to consider how I might be able to release myself with that, and yes, the idea was there; I wasn't sure it would work, but I didn't have a backup plan!

He came back in, ignored his mother, and stood beside me, saying, "I need to give you the booster IV (intravenous) it includes all the vitamins your body needs for carrying a baby, so I should make sure what occurred before doesn't happen again. This time, I want to be in charge, and I also want to be involved with our baby."

I'm not sure when he decided that having a child was so vital to him! I was sure he had stopped taking his pills since he was completely insane!

He appeared strange, as if something had shifted inside him; he was unaware of his time and location, and he was constantly checking his watch, as if expecting someone or something to happen soon. He was plundering his eyes and itching his skull.

He appeared to be extremely emaciated, with no shaven or even showered face, an entirely different attitude, and even a completely different level of insanity. He was conversing with himself, answering his own questions, and smiling or becoming enraged at random intervals.

I asked him to check on his mother, but he ignored me. "I need your help to place the needle in your hand; I've never done it before, but I'm confident that if you help me and don't shake too much, I'll be able to do it easily!" he added.

I was terrified since I had no idea what he was about to inject into my body! "Edwin, if you open your hands, I can help you," I said. "I am not like before, as you can see. I understand that everything you're doing is to keep the future baby safe, so if you trust me, I'll become involved and assist."

I had no idea I could fool him in this way, but I was certain he was still smitten with me and making myself more sweetheart was the only thing that came to me at the time.

He was initially taken aback and hesitant to trust me, but he couldn't deny his feelings for me, so he made a move and opened both of my hands.

My legs were still tethered to the bed by a heavy rope; I couldn't turn but could sit. I put my left hand in front of me and pointed to the vein near my right elbow, telling him that was the one always being utilized.

Obviously, I was exaggerating; I had a very thin vein all the time, and the nurses were fussing about it. They tried a few times until they could do a blood test or give me a standard IV.

He unveiled the needle and tried it at first, but nothing appeared. He even tried it on my hand in the wrong and different directions, which was excruciatingly painful, but I kept quiet because I was aware of my condition.

I had no idea where this much courage came from in my body! Even I was taken aback.

He was irritated and complained about the needle's size, claiming that he was assured of receiving a thin needle, but it was still not the one he desired.

I was bleeding from the locations he was experimenting with since he was in such a hurry that he forgot to cover them with alcohol pads. After a while, I began to cry quietly and gently, hoping to make him feel sorry and stop what he was doing…I needed his full focus.

"Oh, my darling, am I hurting you?" he asked, staring into my eyes.

"Can you offer me a glass of water, I think I've lost a lot of blood," I shook my head and said, then he looked closer and discovered the whole sheet was full of blood.

I hurriedly hid the needle and appeared to be sick while he ran to get a glass of water.

When he returned, finding me sick, he became even more concerned and asked, "Ariana, my darling, what can I do to make you feel better?"

"Please assist me in going to the restroom; I need to clean up and recharge. Since I've lost a lot of blood, maybe eating something sweet may help."

I wasn't feeling well, but there was no time to spare; I needed to get out of that bed.

I was still trying not to look him in the eyes because I was afraid he'd figure out I was acting. He kissed my hand and untangled the ropes from my legs, as well as assisting me in my descent. When I yelled his name when he was facing the other side, he turned his face to me and I smashed into his eyes!

He began to scream and his face was covered in blood; I struck him down with the IV stand on his head; he tried to grab my feet but couldn't see clearly; I repeated the process, this time hitting him harder; eventually, he was knocked unconscious!

Pulled him up onto the bed as quickly as possible and use the ropes to secure his hands and legs to the bed. Carrying him was so painful that I was praying and crying at the same time. I was shivering and my legs were weak.

I knew he wouldn't die easily, but this way, at the very least, I'd be able to find a way out before he got back on his feet. I'm not sure why, but I couldn't finish him; I was too worried about his dying in the situation, and I still cared about him as a human.

Chapter 36
Screaming Green

I had seen him conversing on his smartphone earlier, and I knew it was in his pocket, but I was too afraid to search him; what if he had opened his eyes!

I convinced myself that I had to finish it because I had come so far and there was no turning back.

I looked in his pocket and discovered it; I had no idea how to use it, but I knew the police number, so I tried a few times until it worked.

I told them to send their team right away and that I would explain everything I could; I knew he was going to wake up soon and that relying on the cops would not be a smart idea, so I had to act.

He never dreamed I'd escape again, so he opened the hall door; otherwise, he would have shut all the doors, windows, and gates, just as before.

I went to Ms. Elsa and attempted to contact her several times, but she didn't answer, and there were no heartbeats, therefore she was regretfully gone.

I dashed downstairs and out the door. I didn't know what time it was, but the sky was still bright, and the main gate was locked, so I went up the tree, leapt on the wall, and landed on the floor, like I had done before.

On my feet, I was injured by broken glass…But it didn't sway me for a second; on the way, I had to pull over because I was vomiting; what had he fed me? I was dizzy and my power was dwindling when I saw police cars and started screaming and waving at them…

I awoke and looked around; everything was white; I saw my mother near my bed; I thought I was dreaming; she walked over and took my hand, crying, and said: "Ariana, you are safe, please wake up, I am so scared," I said as I inquired about my whereabouts. and she explains that when the police discovered me on the road, I was immediately taken to the hospital.

I looked down at my hand and noticed that I had been given an IV, so I asked my mother, "Did they catch him? Please, say yes, Mom."

"Yes, he is with police, they have him," she replied as she moved closer and took my arm in hers.

I opened my eyes wider and asked her, "So he is not dead?"

"Unfortunately, no," Mom said with a shake of her head.

I had been in the hospital for two days, and I was eager to return because my classes were about to begin. I believe I was used to getting harmed and then standing up and returning to my normal routine.

My father was also present, and he requested that I stay longer if necessary.

Mom informed me that she had contacted Ms. Marble and invited her to pay me a visit. She wanted to know if there was any reason why I might miss my classes.

I didn't tell anyone about it because the only thing on my mind was getting back to university.

Mom and Dad were not talking to one other, but they both wanted to show how worried they were in that room.

I had to respond to a number of questions from police officers and detectives…

Sadly, Ms. Elsa was discovered dead, her wounds horribly infected. I was very frustrated that I was unable to assist her in a timely manner. Imagine her in her lovely party gown, holding her husband's hand as she walks up and down the hall.

When I asked where Ms. Elsa's husband was, they said they didn't know, but that they had discovered one burned body in the basement of the old house. They're conducting testing to determine who owns it, but they're presuming it's him.

The hospital room was set up like a job interview, with one group entering and another departing with their notebooks in hand.

Dr Lili arrived alone this time, with no one to accompany her. Seeing her in the hospital was not at all pleasant. She asked that no one bother us, and she was not pleased to see me on the bed. I didn't want anybody to know I was visiting a psychologist, particularly my family.

"I'm sorry, but the police phoned me out of nowhere and asked me to explain your situation to them," she added as she pushed a chair in front of her. "They must have known Edwin would return to you, because they have been recording everything and spying on you in order to contact Edwin."

"At least, they have him now," I informed Lili.

When she asked whether I needed to talk about it, I opened the bandage around my neck and said, "Nothing much to say, you can see it for yourself."

"Ariana, you have been through a lot in this age," she added after covering her face for a few seconds. I believe you should take some time off and recover.

Returning to university will not compensate for what has happened to you.

"I need to keep myself occupied, I need to return to my studies, this is the only thing that will calm me down, I don't have a proper family anymore, all is gone, all that is left for me is my eternal goal," I explained.

She was still unhappy with my response, but I assume she understood what I was expressing when she replied, "I will inform Ms. Marble; you will resume your courses, but I need to see you more frequently in my position."

I thanked her and she exited the room; I was exhausted from all of the discussions and closed my eyes to sleep.

The next day, my parents escorted me to the dormitory, where Ms. Marble was waiting for me. She came up to my parents and said, "I will stay at her side and if anything is needed, I will alert both of you."

Before saying good-bye, my father said something to me that I wish he had kept to himself for the time being, at least until I was better…"There is something you should know, and the sooner I say it, the better," he added. "Edwin has transferred all of his assets to you, and Ms. Jane was informed yesterday by the society of which you are a member. She assured me that once you are okay, she can meet you and talk about it. Now you are one of the wealthiest individuals in the city."

I wasn't surprised at all to hear something like that, but my mother was! I suppose she was about to scream since her mouth was wide open. "Do you guys want to go to the family hall, which I can organize right away?" Ms. Marble interjected.

"There is nothing to discuss, I am drowsy, please allow me to go to my room," I hastily said.

Father apologized and hugged me, though Mother remained stiff and forced herself to say goodbye.

Ms. Marble had prepared a meal for both of us and asked if we might eat it in my room; I was not in the mood, but it would be rude to refuse.

I had some time to shower and change before she prepared the dinner on two plates and brought it to my cabin; I was hungry so I chose to eat first.

"I was forced to marry a guy at the age of fifteen, my family sold me to an old man who was about fifty years older than me, and I was his servant and wife at the same time," she explained. I was pregnant when he died, and his children and family kicked me out of the house. Imagine being pregnant without food or shelter, and my family didn't welcome me anymore.

They couldn't afford to look after me since they didn't have enough money. One day, a woman and her daughter were coming down the street when they noticed me sitting on the payment, pregnant and begging for money!

They were my angels; they gave me shelter till my daughter was born, then got me a place to live and work, as well as assisting me in finishing high school. "Those two angels are Lili and her mother."

"Ariana, life has been unfair to so many of us, I can easily understand the pain and hatred in your eyes," she remarked, wiping away tears. "However, all of this will pass. There will be wonderful times in your life as well; God is watching us and examining the ones who are most important to him; don't lose faith."

I was taken aback by her narrative and felt terrible for her having to go through it all at the age of fifteen! Because she saw me in this scenario, she must have felt compelled to share her tale with a student like myself; otherwise, I would have known it was not permitted.

We were telling similar stories, but from different points in time. I wish I could go back in time and erase my memories. I was feeling suffocated...There was no laughter, and there were no tears!

Chapter 37
Antique Brass

I didn't know what to wear, and there was a bus waiting outside to transport students to their classes, and I was the last one to board.

Elena approached me in class and hugged me, saying that with the scarf around my neck, I had become more perfect!

"In my holidays, I met Sir Malik, I don't know if you are familiar with Art, if yes, you should surely know him, he is the finest, and I managed to take some private classes with him," Mohamad remarked, handing over a book full of Arts copies. I figured you could treasure this book because that is how I fell in love with his work: there's a history of each of his paintings under each one.

I'd never received a book as a present before, so that was thoughtful of him.

Elena became jealous and asked, "Would you have gifted me too if I was as attractive as her?"

"Just for the record, you are incredibly lovely, but in a different way," Mohamad added with a giggle.

Elena glanced at me and we both smiled at the same time; I believe it was the first time I had smiled since my tragedy. I thought to myself, *I'll never smile again. I'd be lying if I said I wasn't missing Mr. Farhad in First Class, but how could a lady like me be with a man like him? I don't deserve to be loved again; the most I can hope for is the pleasure of conversing with him.*

I could feel his heavy gaze on me, as if he was missing me and couldn't stop staring; Elena turned around and said, "I told you, Ariana, even Mr. Farhad can't stop himself with that scarf around your neck."

The name of the scarf jiggled in my memory; a reminder of whose name was on the neck label. I was very careful with the scarf during class since I was concerned it would fall. I had no choice but to act.

I recall the doctor telling me in the hospital that there was a procedure in extracting skin from my leg and transplanting it to my neck, but that it would take a long time to recuperate.

After class, I went straight to my cabin, where Ms. Marble was waiting for me. I hurriedly changed into my pajamas because she had placed an order for pizza and said that she couldn't cook since the gas cylinder had run out.

We just talked about the usual stuff, and when I started drowsy, she told me to go to bed early due Dr. Lili was waiting for me the next day.

I went to bed, almost closed my eyes, when the phone rang, it was him, how could I not know?

"Hello, Mr. Farhad, how are you?" I asked, as if it was my first time speaking with him.

"Hello, dear friend," he said, "before I begin, I felt so lonely while you were away; it is challenging to get through the holidays without a friend."

Then he inquired about Arta and my family, to which I replied that everything was OK except for the tragedy.

He also stated that he and his lawyer had gone through a large number of files and that he was able to complete a large number of unfinished assignments.

"Can I ask you a question, Arianna?"

"Obviously yeah," I replied, "please tell me."

"I've started to have a feeling about you, and I'd like to know whether we're on the same page? Is it okay if I fall for you? Do you think we'll be able to be more than just colleagues one day?"

Oh, gash, I burst out crying at that point; I had been holding in and managing my emotions all along, but this was out of my control; it was my heart…my damaged heart…

He became concerned and apologized; I said that I had a big day ahead of me and that I would be happy to address his question later, when I was feeling much better.

I believe he was offended by his own question, so he quickly apologized and said, "I'm sorry, I wasn't thinking clearly, as you have noticed, this is my first experience falling for a girl, and I'm not very good at it."

"You are correct; it is best for you to rest, and we will speak again soon." He instantly ended the call without waiting for my response.

I envisioned myself beside him, laying on his shoulder, trying to bury myself in his arms, and murmuring in his ear, "I'm falling for you too." I desired his adoration because it was so fresh and pure. I wanted him to be my man and give me the attention I deserved, but I couldn't…

The next day, I went to see Dr. Lili, who was as cheerful and pleasant as ever. She poured me a cup of green tea and, after a brief discussion about Ms. Marble and their friendship, she began asking me to empty my mind by recounting the day Edwin kidnapped me.

Why should I keep talking about such a horrible thing over and over again, I wondered. I informed her that I preferred not to discuss it.

"Ariana, I signed your release papers, and I asked the police to let you return to your classes in exchange for me curing your anger and going over your past with you, because they believed you might be a threat to society," she stated. "I know this isn't what you were expecting from me, but I'm also stuck in an unwelcome situation."

"Are you clear on what that means? If the university or any of your students report a single accident, they can easily put an end to your career."

"Ariana, Edwin has said, all of the crimes, you have been aware of, even your grandmother's, particularly your friend's death," she continued as she sat down next to me on the sofa. "Because of how you feel about him, you haven't said anything."

"You were lying to your parents and eager to do anything with him," he added. "You knew about the old house, which indicates that's where you two have been planning all your murders and doing dirty things with one other!"

I couldn't hear any longer and began to cry, wanting to leave her room. She requested me to remain and calm down, then told me that I may leave if I wished.

After a time, I began conversing and telling her everything, and she began recording my voice because she was required to play for the cops. This was my time to say all I had been worrying about.

I explained to her why I was not speaking to my parents and how I was being forced toward him against my will. I told her how many times I intended to leave him, but my mother persuaded that we should keep going because he was our final chance.

"I was crying all day and all night, like a young girl trying to hide behind my books. Because of Edwin, my father abandoned my mother, my sister moved out of the city, and my younger brother ended himself in rehab.

"How could I possibly be a part of Edwin's plan? He stole my best friend away from me, and my grandmother begged him to leave me alone. He was a wild creature. How many times did I end up in the hospital because of him? He didn't have mercy in his heart, and he took advantage of me. Both sides were putting pressure on me.

"I couldn't stop crying though since my heart was so heavy," I explained. "I went under the protection of CCWR (Community Care of Women Rights) to help me get to university since my family was no longer protecting me, and my mother, who was blind at the time, sold my soul and the spirits of her family to a sick rich boy."

She handed me a drink of water and pressed the recorder's pause button. "I know, you are innocent," she replied after a few seconds, "but I have to show it to them as well, since once he transferred all of their family fortune to you, it caused the police to have doubts about you."

I told her about Farhad, who had expressed his feelings for me the day before. When she asked if I felt the same way, I responded, "I am full of mess, dirt, and a bad past, how can I fall in love again?"

"Perhaps it is too early to talk about love with you right now, because you are still fighting with the first one," she continued, "but I am confident that very soon these all will be over and you will find love again, and I mean true love, and whoever wants you will accept your past as well."

She added that someone has volunteered to take my case and assist me with all of the accusations, and that Edwin's first court appearance is coming up next week, which I will have to attend as the single witness to the crime.

I was anxious about going to court, but she assured me that the lawyer is a well-known figure who would not allow them to bother me.

Farhad didn't call that night, and I was expecting to hear his voice. I was convinced, he was still angry with me…I knew Mom and Dad hadn't told Arta about the incident since when she called, she seemed normal. I wished I hadn't been Ariana that night and that my misfortune had been different.

Chapter 38
Electric Lime

My classes continued, and Farhad never phoned back after that night; the only calls I received were from my family, which was not very often.

Farhad tried not to make eye contact with me in class, but he couldn't help himself sometimes…

On the day of the hearing, I was instructed to arrive two hours early so that the lawyer could speak with me before the testimony began.

My father and Dr. Lili were also present, but I begged my mother not to go since I was not sure she would be pleased with the things I or others would say about her.

Dr Lili, my father, and I were waiting in the family hall for the lawyer to arrive when a young guy entered carrying paperwork and a large bag. "Are you the one who is going to present my daughter?" said father.

The stranger then proceeded to step up to the front and introduce himself. No, I work in his office, and he'll be right here, he added with a smile.

When the door opened and he stepped in, I was so taken aback that I leapt to my feet and dropped my purse. "Mr. Farhad, what are you doing here?" questioned father, who also rushed to the front and shook his hand.

He said hello to everyone before saying, "I'm going to present Ms. Ariana's case."

Dr. Lili had never met Farhad before, and she had no idea he was the person I had mentioned. I was still stunned, wondering why he was here and why he was the one who should represent me out of all the other lawyers.

Then he began to describe how and why he became involved. "I mainly aided young adults who were stuck in situations where they couldn't get out without the assistance of a lawyer. As you are aware, I am Ariana's university Master, and approaching Human Resources and obtaining approval for her case was not easy.”

“He’s been your master all this time, and you haven’t said anything,” Dad remarked, looking at me.

“There was no reason to explain anything, sir,” Dr Lili said, smiling, “since in their age, they don’t like to reveal many things, especially after what she has gone through, you may allow her the right to be silent, it is completely different from a high school.” She wanted to put on a show for me.

He told my father, “I will make sure they don’t trouble her at all, this is a very clear case and I don’t think it would be necessary for her to go any more after today, I will be here and please don’t worry, everything are going to be OK,” following a little chat and explanation of how this would work.

After that, he requested his assistance in facilitating Dr Lili and my father in entering the main hall, while he desired to be alone with me.

After everyone had left, he asked me to take a seat closer to him, which I declined and questioned him, “So you were working for the cops all these days? Was it simply your duty to keep us awake all those nights on the phone? Didn’t you think I deserved the truth?”

“Please don’t mess things up; let me explain how I ended up in this situation.”

“After the first day of my lesson with you, I got a call from the detective who was investigating your case, querying about you, and what was my history with your family,” he added, pulling a tissue from his pocket and wiping the sweat off his brow.

“When I found out why they were after you, I wanted to help, and knowing what he has done to you and your family has driven me to keep going until I am able to rescue you from him. I felt terrible since I was the one who had stolen your home away from you.”

“Unfortunately, one day before the holidays ended, I found about him kidnapping you and all the other things he did to his parents. I volunteered to assist you since I couldn’t sit and keep quitting any longer. To obtain their approval, I went through a lot at the university. I just needed to be by your side. Ariana, I am here to protect you, not as your master, but as a friend, as a person, as a lawyer, as a lover,” he replied, his eyes narrowing. “My emotions for you haven’t altered, and I’m willing to give up my university career in order to focus only on my court job because of you.”

"It doesn't matter to me if they take my mastership away from me. I've found someone in my life who has given me happiness and peace, and even if you reject me, I'm not going to let you go."

"I'm doing this for myself, not for you; I'm trying to show myself how deeply I can care about someone; please don't put too much pressure on yourself; in exchange, you don't have to love me. I don't expect anything from you or your folks."

I was at a loss for words, staring at him, trying to disguise my emotions, while on the other hand, I was irritated with myself for not trusting him from the start.

Then he began going over my case with me, telling me that if anything was missing, I should let him know right away before we entered the hall.

We were soon in the courtroom, and my hands were shivering. I believe he sensed and softly placed his hands on my shoulders without anyone noticing.

Edwin was brought in with his wounded eye covered, and he could only see with one eye. They instructed him to stand in front of everyone and present himself. I was looking down, trying to avoid him.

Then the questions started coming in one by one, and both lawyers were answering. Some questions should have been answered immediately by me and him as well. His lawyer did not appear to be attempting to work on the case; I believe he was presenting him because he had no other option.

When compared to his previous appearance, Edwin appeared to be a complete transformation. Once upon a time, I was over heels in love with him and delighted about my choice. Take a peek at where we are right now!

Edwin's internal smile was obvious on his face every time he gazed at me. The court took two hours, and the judge soon announced that we will all find out what would happen to this case the coming day.

Farhad was not happy with the way he was looking at me, and I could see how furious he was getting, so I encouraged him not to get concerned with his craziness and focus on the case.

I wished I didn't have to return to my cabin, but I didn't have any other options. I needed someone to talk to, someone like Catherine, who wasn't a cop, a lawyer, or a doctor.

Before leaving, my father walked up to me and held me, saying, "Please, Ariana, start sharing your thoughts and emotions with your family, just because your mother and I are separated, doesn't mean we aren't there for you or don't care what happens to you."

I knew he was still irritated that I hadn't told him about Mr. Farhad, but I didn't know how to tell my family about him. They already disliked him since he instructed them to leave the building.

"Everything proceeded the way I imagined it would," Dr Lili stated, smiling. "My dearest, we'll meet again, and I'm sure we'll have a lot to chat about now that I know who Farhad is!"

Then she blinked and left. I planned to take the bus back to my room, but Farhad asked if he could give me a ride, which I declined.

"Our friendship has taken on a new face; now I can't think of you the way I used to; I'm under pressure whenever I look into your eyes; I have feelings for you as well; however, after all of this, I'm not sure it's advisable for us to continue; I'm sorry if I didn't tell you anything about him; however, I was happy to be with you, not worried about how you judge me."

Then I immediately thanked him for everything and dashed to the bus stop…

He remained standing and smiling as he looked at me, then sat in his car and drove up to the bus stop, got out, and said, "I will inform you about the outcome of the case, no need for you to attend the hearing. And I'll consider your word as a yes to my love."

He was as joyful as ever, and he got in his car and drove away.

Chapter 39
Burnt Sienna

Everything returned to normal the next day; my classes were in session, and everyone was gearing up for exams. I couldn't because I was too concerned about the court's decision.

I was ready for Farhad to attend the class at any point and startle me with the final.

I couldn't wait any longer, so I dropped the last class of the day, which was in the late afternoon, and immediately returned to my Cubin.

Ms. Marble was also not in her room; I had Farhad's number; however, I didn't want to call him as I knew every step I made would be controlled by the cops.

I had a shower, and as soon as I was out of the house, the phone rang, which I instantly answered. Farhad was not pleased; he seemed dissatisfied, and after asking how my day had gone and a few inquiries regarding my health, he said, "Edwin is being given the death penalty since the other body that was burnt also related to his father, therefore the judge reached his decision without hesitation, and it will be performed out this coming Friday."

I was relieved, so he would finally disappear for good, but I couldn't figure out why Farhad was so irritated! "Is there anything more you want to tell me that's bothering you?" I inquired.

"Edwin has requested if he can meet you for the last time, and that has been his farewell wish, and the worst portion is that the court has accepted," Farhad responded.

"That means I have to go seated in front of him; he'll definitely kill me this time; I'm certain that he has a plan, which is why he's asked for this," I explained.

Farhad was irritated as usual. "I spoke to the judge and asked him not to allow such a thing, but he said there will be no problem since there will be police guards in the room."

"Now it's entirely up to you whether you want to join him or not," he continued.

I was silent, or perhaps I was thinking, Farhad was becoming increasingly irritated as I remained silent. "Ariana," he inquired. "Do you want me to reject it on your behalf?"

I wished I could say yes and put an end to it all, but I wasn't sure, and I even astonished myself by telling Farhad, "I'm terrified, but there will be a security, as the judge indicated, so I have a sense I should go there one last time, we need closure."

Farhad took a bit longer this time to respond, "Sure, I can understand, and I apologize if I was thinking emotionally." As a result, the date has been set for Friday, two hours before the execution.

"Would you be there too?" I questioned him, still unsure if I wanted to do it.

"It's my responsibility to be there, I'm your lawyer," he explained, "but I won't be permitted into the room."

I wanted to say something to calm his outrage and assure him that I am attempting to do the right thing, so I added:

"As long as you're there, I'm sure I won't be worried," I said, adding, "and thanks, Farhad, for doing all of them for me."

He was surprised to hear his name, which I believe made him happy. He asked me to come to class the next day because he missed me, I was sure he was smiling as he hung up the phone.

With two days till Edwin's sentencing, I was not at ease, or perhaps afraid that he might escape. I knew it was wrong to say it, but I won't be able to rest until I bury his remains in the earth.

I had to phone my father and inform him of Edwin's final desire; he was furious, but Ms. Jane assured me that she would make him understand; why did I have to do that?

For the same reason, I called my mother. She was irritated that I wouldn't let her attend court.

When I told her about Mr. Farhad, she became agitated and began yelling. After a while listening to her, I told her that if she continued to act in this manner, I would never call her or speak to her again!

She suddenly gathered herself and apologized, "Sorry, I got a little carried away at the start, so damage is already done, at least he is attempting to assist now."

I also informed her that I would be visiting Edwin prior to his execution. She warned me not to approach him since he was clearly up to something.

"Everything would be alright," I convinced her.

That day, I took a taxi to the central prison, where Farhad awaited me. I wasn't sure if I was dressed appropriately. He was more worried than I was. We passed through several security gates before arriving at the one where Edwin was stationed.

"Ariana, are you sure you want to do this?" Farhad questioned.

"Let's finish it," I replied with a smile.

When the gate opened, I noticed three guards standing in the room, each in a different position, and Edwin seated in the chair with his hand and leg cuffs on.

I was standing and didn't want to approach him; however, when he noticed me, he stood up, said hello, and moved for me to find a seat. I walked over to where the security guard was located and sat down.

"I never knew one day would arrive in my life, seeing you will be my final hope!" he replied with a smile. "You were cursed, and your love for me was poisonous."

"Is that all?" I asked.

He replied, "I told everyone about the things you did, Adriana, but no one believed me. I don't suppose you'll get along with it."

"We have a lot in common. Everything my family has worked for is now yours; this is why you came to me in the first place; perhaps if your love had been pure, it would have transformed the dark side of me. If you and your mother needed money, you could simply ask instead of playing. I wish you would have destroyed me that day, I wanted to die with your wonderful loving memory, not this way, knowing what a disgusting person you have become into." He was nearly yelling.

When the guard instructed him to keep it low, I realized this was the moment I needed to speak up. It was my turn to open up about my old wound, even though I knew telling him wouldn't change anything in his dark heart.

"When I met you, I was a small girl who had no idea what boyfriend meant, nor did I have any idea what it meant to use marijuana, be drunk, or get high!

"I was the one who was embarrassed to look in the mirror when she was necked, but you taught me how to take off my clothing, stand in front of the camera, and pose in the best figure I could, as these images sold the most!

"You horrible beast took away my grandmother, my best friend, my family fell apart, and my brothers ended up in rehab. Everything was taken away from us.

"You were like an animal, just didn't know when to stop, spoilt rich boy, didn't know the worth of anything, so please shut your mouth and go to hell, because you don't belong here. You were a terrible mistake of her life, your mother used to say."

I shouted all of that while crying, unable to hold on to my hatred any longer. My chest was heavy, I couldn't breathe, and these were the only things I could say to him.

"See you in hell, my love, my ghost will chase you, this is just the new begging for our unfinished love story," he shouted as he exited.

When the gate opened, I cried and requested Farhad to take me to my cabin. He took me to the family room and asked me to calm down, not saying anything and allowing me to release all of my frustration.

"Sir, it is time, and we must be there," his assistant stated as he entered the hall.

He winked at me and said, "I'll go; you don't need to attend the final chapter of evil's life."

Then he requested his assistant to escort me to his car and wait with me until he returned.

I got in the car and sat down, but I was cold in the middle of a warm day! I grabbed Farhad's coat beneath the seat, put it on, and closed my eyes, feeling as if I hadn't slept properly in two years.

When I opened my eyes, I found myself in front of the dormitory, looking around and saw Farhad smiling at me and saying, "Just on time, I tried to drive gently so you could sleep longer. I'm not permitted to carry you in; this small way, dear lady, you must walk."

"Is it over, Farhad, has he given up?" I inquired, wiping my eyes.

"Yes, everything is finished; in fact, I stayed a little longer to double-check." I witnessed every operation since he wanted that his body be cremated.

Everything was completed. "You are now free."

Chapter 40
Purple Heart

My days returned to normal, lessons resumed, and as previously stated, tests were scheduled one after another, with no time to spare.

This time, I had to put more effort to the courses since I missed a few sessions then had to read and study them on my own. It was far from simple.

Elena and Mohamad were studying at the library with me, and it was different since they were quite helpful. I also noticed that there was much more than friendship between them, which made me glad.

The university was about to close for the summer, and I needed to decide where I wanted to stay.

Farhad was phoning every night, wanting to have a good time with me. He was a true gentleman, not once reminding me of my past or attempting to open up about Edwin.

He was asking me to let him to meet my parents, and this time he was asking for their permission to marry me. I was not ready, and I kept coming up with excuses to avoid it. He was more worried about losing me than anything else.

I knew how he felt about me, but I wasn't so sure about myself! He was exactly who I had always imagined, but I had met him during a very tough period in my life.

He desired love, life, and a wife, whereas I desired to stay alone, miserable, and depressed!

I began to see Dr. Lili more frequently, especially while I was also under exam pressure, because it was impossible to carry that much stress at the same time.

She was attempting to allow me to express my thoughts about Farhad or even my childhood, as well as my connection with my parents, mainly my mother.

I couldn't expect anything more from her because she'd been trying to do her job, and I wasn't going to tell her everything because I knew she had to report everything to the cops. These were several formal sessions that we were required to attend by the court.

I decided to meet Ms. Jane after my finals and go through the property and wealth that Edwin had left for me.

Ms. Jane was very helpful, and since she had become my stepmother, she was much more understanding, therefore I liked her even better than before.

She explained me my options and requested me to make an informed decision. She also offered me to employ three lawyers, because the job could not be completed by one.

Edwin's family owned several properties, bank accounts, and interests in various parts of the country and abroad. In order to obtain more information, the lawyer attempted to communicate with their references and authorities.

It took them a few weeks to collect all of the information that we required.

I decided to name a hospital after my grandma, as well as a large high school for girls in our town after Catherine. I also helped Catherin's family financially.

I made a significant donation to cancer patients and their families.

I also sent Ms. Jane a check for CCWR (community care of women's rights) to support those girls who are similar to me and to try to build the community by letting more people know about such an institution.

My name was soon in every newspaper and magazine, I was named the fourth richest person in the country, and I was getting extra attention because I was single!

Farhad was not pleased with this, and he insisted on meeting with my father before I left for the summer vacation.

With only one week till the end of the semester, everyone was packing and preparing. Elena insisted that I go to their farmhouse in the countryside and stay with her for a few days, but I wasn't even in the mood.

Ms. Marble came into my room one night and asked if we could have one last meal together.

I was overjoyed to see her because, since the whole idea of me becoming wealthy came up, I had rarely spent time with her and was usually busy with attorneys and running around cities.

I was used to her meals since it was similar to my mother's.

"Ariana, what do you want to do with all that money?" she said after dinner. "You're still coming back and sleeping in janitor's little room, and you don't even have your own smartphone despite your wealth. I sense something is wrong with you these days, could you perhaps talk to me?"

"Oh Ms. Marble, I'm so grateful you care about me, because I've been asking myself the same question for a long time and I don't know if I'll ever be okay, I don't know who I am or even what I am anymore?"

"I've always wanted to go to university; it was a dream of mine, but my family, particularly my mother, had a different ambition."

"I don't feel like it's me any longer, once I fell in love, since it was a bad decision, it ripped my family away from me, and today I have everything I've ever wanted in life, but I'm not happy.

"I have lost my only friend, and it has been extremely difficult for me to form new friendships with anyone else since then. I am afraid that someone will kill her too in revenge of me. I'm nineteen years old, but I feel like I've lived the life of a sixty-year-old lady."

Ms. Marble brought me a glass of water and requested me to sip while trying to hide her tear.

"Edwin cursed me by bestowing his fortune upon me; now my parents, sister, her husband, and all of our friends and their families want me to begin paying for everything. Everyone expects something from me, but no one realizes that this isn't my money, and I don't own it," I explained.

"What about Mr. Farhad, don't you believe you deserve a fresh start with someone who is committed to his love?" Ms. Marble inquired after hearing about my relationship with him. "Why don't you attempt to put everything behind you and just live in the moment? He sounds like a kind guy with a good background," she spoke.

"I'm tired, I've lost my feelings, I didn't have time to mourn for my grandmother, Catherine, or my broken family, not even my injured and wounded body!" I answered. "Everything happens at the same time."

"It was my dream to attend university, and all of these things have happened to me because I wanted to study, and now that I am here, I haven't even had a chance to celebrate my achievement."

"You are correct."

"Farhad is a nice case and a good person to begin with, but the problem is that I am not good, and I am still haunted by my past. He showed up at the wrong time, and I wished I could freeze the moment, wipe the darkness from the past, and start over with him."

Ms. Marble stated she had an idea but wasn't sure if I would like it after a while of discussion.

"I used to visit a friend who lives in an area called Mountain of Angels with my daughter. This place is so calm, there is no electricity and people use candles to brighten their houses, and the atmosphere is always lovely. There is a legend that whoever comes to this area with a broken heart will be healed by the angels of the mountain, and there have been many miracles.

"I know these are old people's beliefs or maybe foolishness, but you don't have much to lose right now, and you're seeking for a somewhere to clear your thoughts, so take advantage of the opportunity and spend your summer there alone," she stated.

I had never considered leaving and discovering about this area made me chuckle.

Chapter 41
Rainbow

My clothing were basically party outfits; therefore, I didn't have much to pack. I chose to travel by bus as I just had some few cash in my pocket. It was merely a five-hour drive to the place. Ms. Marble estimated that getting to the peak of the mountain would take another hour.

When I told my family, my father was furious, and my mother questioned why I needed to visit such uncivilized castles when I was so wealthy.

"Ariana, it is not easy to let you go after what happened to you last trip," he said, "but if this is what you want, I won't stop you." I had to visit Farhad before going to the terminal since he wasn't convinced going to the mountain was a good idea.

"Farhad, there are things I need to clear with myself, and I think after everything I've been through, I deserve a break," I thanked him. "I need to get away; I'm not sure how long I'll be able to stay there, but I'd want to give it a shot. I'm not sure why I'm heading there, but I need responses."

He wished me happiness and assured me that the next time he sees me, he must know I am alright.

I had to leave quickly because my ticket was for nine a.m., and the bus was packed. I was grateful for a single seat next to the window.

I couldn't sleep because I was so thrilled; I didn't know where I was going or who I was going to see; all I had was the name and address of Ms. Marble's friend.

It was always fun to sit next to the window, and after a few hours, we arrived at our destination. It was a little village with only a few stores and, I believe, one restaurant.

I went to the tiny market and bought a packet of biscuits, and when I was checking out, I asked the lady behind the counter if she knew somebody named

Diva, and she grinned and replied, "Ms. Diva is very well-known in our area, and everyone who visits wants to meet her." Then she showed me how to get to the top of the mountain, where she was.

My guide to her house was a small boy. He continued telling me how tall and gorgeous I was, which I took as a compliment, but he was way too young to start flirting with a girl my age!

Finally, we arrived; the view from above was breathtaking; I had never expected to see so much beauty at once; the fresh air filled my lungs, and the cool breeze on my face seemed like someone was gently massaging my cheeks.

Ms. Diva has a healing skill, according to the boy, and there are many stories about her.

"She came here from India with her husband many years ago, and she was so unlucky that her husband fell down from the mountain, that she never returned, and he made that area her home," he spoke.

"Also, some believe her spouse left her there forever and gone, but no one knows the truth because she doesn't like to share her story," he added.

"People believe the angels in the mountains have helped her survive in such a harsh environment for all those years," he clarified.

He showed me her house and then went; I was confused and looked at myself and where I was standing; I began to wonder why I was here and if I truly believed in this foolishness that most people make up to fill their pockets.

Suddenly, the gates opened, and I saw an elderly lady dressed in a white gown, who appeared to be in good health, calling out to me, "Are you going to come with me or do you want to keep staring at me?"

"I know who you are, and you are very welcome at my cottage," she hugged me and said. "Marble is my good friend, she has a lovely heart, and I can't say no to any of her requests, and her friends are also my friends."

I couldn't believe there was a river running through her hall or that she had built her bedroom around the trees as she showed me around her house, which was a large garden at the top of the mountain.

"This one is yours now, I don't have much but everything I have is yours too," she said as she showed me my room. "Please rest and I'll see you in an hour for dinner, I have a habit of eating at six in the evening."

I thanked her and quickly proceeded to shower and clean myself before coming to lay down on the bed. I felt weird, as if I wasn't myself anymore, but it felt nice this time.

I walked to the hall and was looking for a dining table when she called me and said, "I don't have it, you'll have to sit on the ground and eat, exactly like in the old days, I hope you don't mind."

"I have been eating all of my meals on the ground in my room with Ms. Marble, so I am entirely fine with it," I said with a smile.

She had prepared some breads, which she referred to as roti, as well as a potato curry, which I assumed had been flavored with Indian spices.

She prayed before eating and invited me to join her in the prayer, which I gladly accepted.

The meal was delicious, and I wished I could have eaten more, but I restrained myself. I assisted her with the dishes, and she handed me a glass of hot goat milk and invited me to accompany her to the garden, where the weather was bitterly cold but beautiful.

"Everyone is coming from different regions around the world to visit a crazy person like me, with many stories has been said about her, sometimes I just don't want to open the gates or if I did, I would end up answering all types of questions," she remarked as we sat on the wooden seat.

She requested me to go to bed early after we talked about her lifestyle and daily routines; she seemed to work with the sun's schedule, and there was no electricity in the house.

She urged me not to be afraid of wolves howling at night because they are harmless to us. I was nervous, but she assured me not to be concerned, so I thanked her again for having me, and she led me to my bed.

I didn't waste any time and went to bed right away.

The next day, I awoke to the sound of singing, changed, went out, and couldn't find her anywhere. I went into the garden and found her amongst the tomato bushes.

"Morning, my dear, you looked like you had a good night, I was picking some tomatoes for our breakfast," she said.

After a delicious breakfast, she told me that as long as I'm there, I need to work, cultivate my own feed, and take care of my expenses.

This doesn't mean I have to pay her, but it does indicate that everything should be done and developed by myself.

There were other things I needed to do and learn, such as how to bake bread or how to cultivate and care for a plant, as well as keep the chicken embryos clean and feed the goats on a regular basis.

There was a lot of training to complete, but I had no idea why I was meant to do it, and I was irritated since I knew it wasn't easy, especially for someone like me who had lived in the city!

She didn't wait for my response and said, "I know it won't be easy, but you will learn a lot and realize the significance of food in addition to working hard to get it in your life."

I never considered it that way, but I suppose she was correct, and a woman her age knew exactly what she was doing, unlike me!

I began following her wherever she went, doing anything she asked of me; it was exhausting, but I didn't realize how quickly time passed, which was excellent, especially for someone like me who didn't want to ponder too much.

My days and nights were practically same, which was good for me because I knew I could leave at any time, but I was curious as to how she had been doing all of this for so long and still seemed so fascinated as if it were her first time.

The same boy who was my mountain guide was also our connection to the outside world, delivering whatever we required and also calling my father to inform him that I was fine.

Ms. Diva and I had a brief discussion virtually every night before we went to bed, and she was usually the one talking while I was listing; she hardly ever asked me any questions about myself.

I wondered whether she cared why I was there, but I preferred to keep quiet and not say anything to her about it; I was trying to get away from what I was, which was why I was there.

Until one day, our guide lad sent a message saying that my mother has been requesting that I call her and that she is concerned.

Honestly, I was annoyed that Ms. Marble had shared my phone number with her! "Please tell her the next time she calls that I am still healthy and very wealthy," I told the boy.

She invited me to one of the rooms where she typically kept her store after he had decided to leave (the guide boy).

Then she gave me an old suitcase and told me to open it. I lightly dust it first. A book, an old perfume bottle, a few pictures, and a Red Silky shall were all found within.

"It belongs to my mother," she remarked, holding the shall in her hand. "My mother was wearing it the day she married."

"Rather than a daughter, my dad was expecting a boy! Around the moment of giving birth to me, my mum passed away! Father didn't want to retain me because I was dubbed Evil, so he placed me in an orphanage. I just have this scarf left over from my mum."

Then she handed it to me and added, "Please feel it; what if this was your mother's only memory? I'm not sure why you told the boy to go tell your mother those things, and I don't care. Just remember that our parents are like rare diamonds that can be taken away at any time."

While cleaning her tears, she sat on the ground and said, "I've spent my entire life imagining how she would have looked, how she would have felt when she hugged me, or how my father would have been; you have no concept what it's like to be an orphan."

She took my hand in hers and motioned for me to sit on the ground as well, while handing me the images and saying:

"This box contains all of my family members, the perfume bottle belonged to my late husband, and this book was given to me by someone dear to my heart.

"Let me tell you a little secret about my life, something I've never told anyone before.

"When I was fifteen, a family approached me and requested me to marry their son and become his second wife. They wanted me to give him a son, as his first marriage had only given him daughters.

"I was in love with a boy at our orphanage, and we told each other that once we reached the age when they allowed us to go, we would marry and have our own family, but that didn't happen, so he gave me these books as a farewell gift."

"Please, if remembering the past makes you upset, stop talking about it." I felt it was necessary to counsel at the moment.

"My history is part of me," she answered, smiling. "Remembering it merely reminds me of how far I've come and how much I've accomplished. I can't ignore it or run away from it; everything that has happened in my life has shaped who I am now; acceptance is the best way to live."

Then we both got up and began walking through the garden, and she kept going. "Some of my husband's relatives who live abroad have assured him that if he comes to this mountain in your land and stays with me for a time, he will definitely have a son!

"We had a long road ahead of us, and the amount of money he and his family spent was insane; we spent a couple of days in the mountains in a little tent!

"He told me at the end of our trip that he had planned the entire trip to get rid of me and that he had never wanted to be with me."

"He urged me to stay here and never go so he could pretend I was dead and carry on with his life and children without me, as well as face his father's concerns about his lack of a son."

She was smiling while speaking, which made me question why she didn't show any regret or sadness!

"For someone like me who was always in the cage, ending up here in the mountain to save his marriage was the finest thing that could have happened to me, and I seized the opportunity. Since then, I've been loving it until now," she stated.

"Various stories have been told about me and my survival on the mountain, as well as my past. As long as they don't butter me, I let them say whatever they want," she continued.

She then asked if I could assist her in preparing our supper.

I wasn't chatting in the kitchen as my mind was preoccupied with what she said about her life and her decision to live in the mountains for so long.

I thanked her for sharing her experience with me after diner and assured her that I would not mention it anyplace.

She stopped me as I was getting ready for bed and asked, "Did I say something to offend you, my dear? I didn't intend it, I only wanted to remind you of how valuable your life is there in front of your eyes."

"No, Ms. Diva, after hearing your story, it made me wonder what I'm running away from. I apologize if I offended you," I told her.

*After that day, I reflected on myself, the events of the day, as well as the people in my life and my future. **It** wasn't easy; there were some parts **I** didn't want to recall, but I forced myself to.*

Chapter 42
Blue Bell

I stayed for another three weeks, keeping myself occupied and pondering my options.

Making a decision seemed simple at the time but sticking to it was nearly impossible.

I wanted to do something that would benefit both myself and others.

Living with Ms. Diva taught me many lessons every day, and seeing her basic life reminded me of something no one had ever taught me before: the significance of safety and happiness.

It began by analyzing my past and revealing details about my mother that I had never considered significant in my life.

She was a hardworking woman who couldn't have a proper date for the rest of her life with my father because she was always too busy doing housework and caring for us and her own mother. She never had true joy or love.

I knew she must have had many dreams for her life when she was my age, but destiny did not grant her every request.

I'm sorry, but I overlooked her hard work and saw just what was in front of my eyes; she didn't mean to hurt me, so she only wanted to do something for all of us, and she reasoned that if me and Edwin married, all of our problems would be solved.

Living with Ms. Diva taught me about life's realities and how they affect us. She merely opened the door to truth in my eyes, causing me to ponder and be grateful more frequently.

I realized how many times I had traveled through the risky zone and survived.

I didn't realize that if it had come to that, I could have easily gone like my friend Catherine or my grandma.

God, on the other hand, wanted me to stay and guided me through all of the difficulties and darkness.

When I looked in the mirror every day, I never noticed or was bothered by the fact that I was labeled on the neck.

Ms. Diva gave me an herbal treatment to massage on my neck, and it clearly worked; my skin began to heal. She said that it had nothing to do with the medicine she prepared, but rather with me and how I was feeling about myself.

I'd had enough of blaming everyone, including myself. I was also a member of the scheme. I could have easily ignored Edwin or told my family the truth about him.

I could have spoken up and told them about his secret location, where he used to take me, but I chose to remain silent and see what the future holds!

While I was there, I began to miss my mother and consider how I could make things right. She, not I, was the one who lost everything! She was depressed and lonely.

It was my responsibility to be there for her, and now was the time to stand by her side and preserve her.

In fact, remembering the past made me feel better about myself. I learned to relax and make room for new experiences. I was chosen to live another day, and I knew it meant I had to accomplish something worthwhile this time.

I began drafting a letter to my mother, informing her about myself and the changes that had occurred in my life. I explained her everything and that I was completely mistaken about our mother-daughter relationship.

There were days when I thought about Farhad and how he came into my life and turned out to be someone who genuinely wanted to be with me.

I got a feeling for him from the moment he stood in front of our gate with his lawyer; he was giving me something I had always desired: confidence. He always supported my decisions, even when they were inappropriate, and let me be me.

I began to notice the positive aspects of him, as well as how hardworking he was. Despite knowing who I was and what had happened to me, he was still willing to stand by me and never condemned me.

I was thinking throughout those days on the phone with him that he was like Edwin, intending to take abuse of me and ultimately hurt me.

After all of these days, I've figured out how to clear my mind and see the truth about everyone. He was only attempting to help me because he knew I was being harmed by another man.

He never asked me to date him, and he never pressured me into a relationship.

I was the one who wanted to hear his peaceful, relaxing speech, yet I was avoiding him.

I was in the mountains for more than six weeks and had no idea how rapidly time had passed. Ms. Diva reminded me that my summer vacation was coming to an end, and it was time to leave before all of the good rooms in the dormitory were taken.

It was the ending of my trip, and it was difficult to leave that atmosphere; Ms. Diva had become a part of my life, and it was difficult to survive without her.

When I asked whether I may visit her again, she smiled and "Ariana, please don't ask this question anymore, you are a modern edition of myself, you brought so much joy to the house and reminded me of my history, you are always welcome sweet heart," she added.

The first thing I did was contribute whatever money Edwin's family had left over to me. That money was not and will never be mine.

I bought a large plot of land outside of town and built hundreds of dwellings there for the homeless.

In addition, I decided to invest in and grow agriculture, purchasing many fields in various regions with the primary goal of employing homeless people.

So, they got a job, a house, and learned something helpful all at the same time.

Whatever they were harvesting was theirs, and if there was any surplus, they were permitted to sell it in the Market for profit.

This is what Ms. Diva taught me, and I attempted to pass it on to others. I was fortunate that the government was willing to assist me.

I decided to hunt for a part-time work in a library near my university. Also, I used my savings to rent a place for my mother, and I spent some weekends with her.

Our relationship was completely different from previously; we were more like friends, and she was incredibly understanding, so I decided to tell her everything that happened in my life.

She was overjoyed and frequently mentioned that a miracle had occurred and that I had returned to her.

Dad and Ms. Jane, who were in love, began touring the country, purchasing a minivan and spending much of their time outside of the city.

Mom had a good relationship with both of them, but it wasn't ideal. She was attempting to accept things in her own unique manner, which I absolutely understood.

Kian is the name of Arta's infant child...She and her family were regularly coming to spend the holidays with us.

When they came, Dad made sure he stayed in town so he could spend as much time as possible with his grandchildren.

Adam was fine and began attending high school; but his father wished to keep him under his supervision, and Ms. Jane was going out of her way to help him reclaim his identity.

Regrettably, he was still rejecting me, but he had a terrific relationship with Farhad, especially since they used to play football together.

Thus, the most significant news of my life: I married Farhad. We chose to marry first, subsequently date and do all the things that people do throughout their engagement period.

I know it was unusual, but we both liked it, and there were numerous advantages for both of us, the most important of which was that we were both happy.

Farhad resigned from his position as a university professor and returned to his office job in order to marry me. I understand it was a significant sacrifice, and I have always appreciated it.

Finally, I'd want to inform you that I now have everything I've ever desired, and I'm enjoying it.

They didn't come easily to me, and I went through a lot of ups and downs.

My faith led me out of the darkness and into the world of beauty; our creator has a plan for everything and everyone; all we have to do now is wait and be patient for the proper time to come.

Love You All,

Ariana